WINTERGREEN

By the same author:

Glad Waters, The Book Guild, 1987
In Danger's Day, The Book Guild, 1995

WINTERGREEN

Scott Cooper

Book Guild Publishing
Sussex, England

First published in Great Britain in 2013 by
The Book Guild Ltd
Pavilion View
19 New Road
Brighton, BN1 1UF

Typesetting in Baskerville by
Keyboard Services, Luton, Bedfordshire

Printed in Great Britain by
CPI Antony Rowe

A catalogue record for this book is available from
The British Library

ISBN 978 1 84624 817 7

To
Pippa and Ted
Without whose loving care
this old codger would never
have had the strength to bring out
this book.

Author's Note

The characters in this story are wholly fictitious, but incidents have been fished out from my subconscious mind, and something vaguely resembling them possibly really did happen.

S.C.

1

'Please, sir, how do you become a virgin?' came a voice in shrill piping tones from the back of the room.

'You'd better ask Matron; she's sure to know,' answered Mike Thornton, form master of the third form. He was displeased with that indomitable female, and this seemed a reasonable way of getting his own back.

It was Stevenson who asked the question, but it wasn't that he really wanted to know the answer. Latin can be a very dull subject when one is ten years old and, according to Mr Williams, the games master, the nearest thing to a future international scrum half that the school has ever produced. He simply asked the first thing that came into his woolly head, anything to stop this 'object goes into the accusative' nonsense which Mr Thornton was explaining so boringly. He rose to go, delighted at the prospect of a lengthy rest from the rigours of 'Wednesday Four', as this particular period was known to all at Wintergreen.

'Not now, Stevenson. Try her after dinner,' said Mike. He was young and inexperienced, but he wasn't falling for that one.

'But, sir, you said...' started Stevenson in an apparently advanced state of indignation.

'Shut up!' said Mike – and he did. The lesson then proceeded with decorum if not with zeal.

Mike was eighteen, and had been at the establishment for one week. In those days, preparatory schools quite often relied on untrained and untested youngsters who did a year's teaching in between public school and university.

1

What is more, these young men frequently made up for their lack of experience by the keenness and zest which they unfailingly displayed. Mike, however, was not the usual type of young gentleman to be a temporary master at a preparatory school like Wintergreen. Not that he wasn't a gentleman, or he wouldn't have been considered. His father went both to preparatory and public schools, and he had greatly appreciated his own school days. However, he refused point-blank to pay through the nose for his son's education when the state was crying out to do it for nothing. Not that he was a mean man: it was just that he genuinely felt that what he saved on Mike's schooling could be more profitably spent on other things. Mike had no difficulty in 'passing' his eleven plus, though the educational pundits did not even then soil their lips with the word – and said exactly the same thing in a dozen longer ones. At his local grammar school, and a mixed one at that, Mike eventually became head boy, with a formidable list of achievements to his credit.

He was a person who thought for himself, and he had a very strong urge to find out what, if anything, he had missed by not going to the preparatory school at which his father had spent five very happy years. Quite off his own bat, he had written to the headmaster, explaining who he was and asking if there was a vacancy on the staff. It so happened that there was, and old Mr Willerby was most impressed by Mike's letter. He summoned him for an interview, feeling that he would at least like to have a look at Thornton's lad. He hardly expected a grammar school boy to speak the Queen's English, they didn't in his young days, but then, he reflected, breeding does count. He was Thornton's son, and Thornton's name appeared twice on the Wintergreen honours board.

Mr Willerby was a headmaster of the old school, nearer seventy than sixty. Even in the 1960s he belonged to a past age. He had a voice of thunder, and he firmly believed in corporal punishment. His boys adored him, which most modern experts would nowadays find extremely puzzling.

'Let me see, now,' he roared after Mike had introduced himself in impeccable English, 'what are your games like?'

'Well, sir,' answered Mike. 'Not too bad. I was cross-country captain and in both elevens.'

'Both elevens? You mean cricket and soccer, I suppose.'

Mr Willerby uttered the word 'soccer' in a tone which conveyed to a nicety his opinion of the game. To him, God was very definitely a rugger player, probably a big second row forward as he himself had been forty years back.

'Yes, sir. One of my contemporaries has played for Arsenal.'

'Do you know anything about rugger?' asked Mr Willerby without much hope.

'Oh, yes, sir. Lad always took me to see at least one home international a year. I haven't played all that much, but I know the rudiments.'

'Good fellow,' said Mr Willerby with evident relief. The last young assistant but three had been heard to say that all balls, whatever their shape, frightened him – he didn't stay the full year.

'Now about the work,' continued Mr Willerby. 'Do you think you can keep my little horrors quiet enough to teach them anything?'

'Unless they are more unruly than small grammar school boys, I am fairly confident,' said Mike.

'They are not,' said Mr Willerby somewhat sourly, and Mike realised that he had put his foot in it.

'Who will I be teaching, sir?' asked Mike quickly.

'Well, I can't let you loose on the Common Entrance and Scholarship boys. You could manage the third form all right, I think.'

'What age are they, sir?'

'They vary considerably. Out of a dozen boys, there will

be the odd bright babe of eight or nine and a couple of elderly duds, but most of them will be ten.'

To Mike, a form of twelve boys seemed very small indeed. For three weeks the previous winter, he had coped with old Blenkinsop's classes at the grammar school, and there were never less than thirty bodies in front of him. After a few more questions, Mike was taken on.

'Come on September eighteenth, the day before the boys arrive,' said Mike's new boss. 'You'll soon get used to our ways. I never could understand why your father didn't send you here as a boy.'

'It was a question of priorities, sir. There wasn't money for everything.'

'Ridiculous. There is no better investment than a good private education.'

'You may well be right, sir. That's what I want to find out for myself. At the moment, I have a completely open mind.'

It was not often that Mr Willerby permitted anyone, least of all a callow young fellow straight from school, to have the last word, but he could think of no suitable rejoinder as Mike took his leave.

Mr Willerby was quite right: Mike did soon get used to the ways of Wintergreen. There were some things that seemed rather odd to him, but he had the good sense neither to expound his views nor to ask out loud the reason why. His only clash with authority was at lunch the day before the opening conversation of this story. Mike was at one end of Matron's table, at which the new boys always sat. Politely but firmly he refused the tapioca pudding which Matron was serving. At the grammar school, where boys bought meal tickets at a shilling apiece, the fussy eater merely did not receive his money's worth if his honourable nose turned up at what was provided. Had tapioca pudding appeared, there would have been many empty plates, for its glutinous consistency is not to everybody's taste.

'What, no pudding!' exclaimed Matron in tones of thunder, which caused a lull in the general conversation. A lesser man than Mike would have changed his mind, hastily, or possibly claimed that Matron had not heard him right.

'No, thank you, Matron,' said Mike in an even tone, tactfully omitting to add that he did not consider it fit for human consumption. He watched the boys being served, and, as they struggled through their helpings, he made a mental note that his decision was the correct one. For him, the matter was closed, but he did not know Matron. She had ruled the school irresistibly for forty years, with an interval of five years' war service with the Wrens, and even Mr Willerby bowed to her iron will.

After the meal, Mike was summoned to her presence by a senior boy, whose conspirational wink proclaimed that he knew just what was coming.

'Hello, Matron,' said Mike breezily, as he poked his head round the door. 'You wanted to see me?'

'Yes. Come here.'

Her tone convinced him than he was on the mat. The quarterdeck manner was unmistakable, and, like many generations of small boys and many ships' companies of Wrens, Mike wilted before her.

'You refused my pudding, Mr Thornton,' she thundered.

'Yes, Matron,' said Mike meekly. Had he been a Wren, he would, have said 'Aye, aye, ma'am' in much the same tone of voice.

'Mr Thornton,' continued Matron. 'The boys must be set a better example. "Eat what is set before you" is the rule at Wintergreen.'

'Yes, Matron,' said Mike, refusing to commit himself to an engagement in which he would be outgunned, outmanoeuvred and inevitably scuppered.

A little of the austerity departed from Matron's voice. This young man might learn. After all, he had not had the advantage of a preparatory school education. It was perhaps ignorance and not open defiance which had caused his astonishing behaviour.

'You see, Mr Thornton,' she said more gently, 'we must make an engineering job of their manners. We can't have faddiness at Wintergreen.'

It should be mentioned that Miss Horatia Blake, Matron in charge of Wintergreen, was the daughter of an engineer rear-admiral. Anything less than an engineering job was to be deplored.

'I apologise, Matron. You will not have me failing you again.'

'That's all right,' continued Matron, endeavouring to adopt a cooing conciliatory tone of voice.

'Do please tell me one thing, Matron,' said Mike, mentally standing at ease.

'Yes, Mike.'

Now that defaulters were over, Matron could be human. It is a tradition in the Service that a senior officer can unbend in the wardroom, even after he has had to deliver the most savage of reprimands.

'What do you yourself think of tapioca pudding?'

Matron was taken aback. Small boys were irrepressible, and she was used to their quick recoveries, but young masters generally had not the strength to come to the surface so soon after her salvos.

'What do I think of it?' she repeated, to give herself time. 'Well, to be quite honest, I think it's absolutely filthy.'

'Then what's the point of forcing it down their poor little throats.'

'The point? Why, it's good training for them. They can't always eat what they like in this world.'

'But that stuff seems a bit drastic,' Mike was forced to plead.

6

'Maybe,' said Matron, 'but I learn a lot from it. If they can take tapioca pudding without wincing, they can take anything. This lot of new boys is an exceptionally good lot. No one was sick.'

Mike could not help but feel that he was glad that this term's young entry was so tough.

It was not until bedtime that Stevenson was able to continue his investigations. He had completely forgotten his interesting query in the Latin lesson, and, had not the Virgin Mary been mentioned at evening chapel, it is probable that he would never have given it another thought.

'Please, Matron...', he started, as his neck was being inspected.

'Wash it again, Stevenson. And no high-water marks next time, or I'll make an engineering job of it myself.'

Stevenson knew that this meant treatment with the pumice stone, and wisely scrubbed decks to their mutual satisfaction.

'That'll pass,' she said.

'Please, Matron,' Stevenson tried again, 'Mr Thornton told me to ask you something.'

When she heard what it was, Matron was not in the least abashed.

'Oh, Mr Thornton did, did he? Well, Stevenson, you'd have some difficulty I'm afraid.'

'Why, Matron?'

'First of all, you'd have to change your sex. It has been done, but not often.'

'Yes, Matron,' said Stevenson.

'You'd have to become a sweet little girl. Would you like that?'

'Ugh!' said Stevenson. 'I wouldn't.'

'And then, you see, you can't become one if you aren't one already.'

'Oh,' said Stevenson. This was all rather difficult.

He hadn't asked 'why', but Matron felt that things should, not be left in the air.

'It's like amateur status, Stevenson. Once you've been paid to play rugby league, you can't become a rugby union international, can you?'

'No, Matron,' said Stevenson. Having every intention of representing England at rugger, and possibly cricket as well, but his interest in virgins was rapidly waning.

'There aren't enough of them in these parts anyway,' continued Matron, as Mrs Williams, who acted as under-matron, hove in sight. From her contours, it was abundantly clear both that she no longer qualified for virgin status and that very shortly she would be looking after her own rather than other people's children. This was a sore point with Matron, who felt that her assistant should have been replaced this term rather than next.

It may be thought that Stevenson was permanently left with the muddled picture of a kind of female rugger player not yet signed on by Rochdale Hornets, but his friend Anderson, a farmer's son, cleared it up for him that night in the dormitory.

'A virgin,' he explained, 'is a sort of human heifer who hasn't yet been put to the bull.'

'Then why couldn't Matron say so?' was Stevenson's comment. He had stayed on Anderson's farm, and knew exactly what he was talking about.

When Matron next met Mike, she told him that he must learn to answer difficult questions, and not worry her with them.

'But I'd never do it so well,' answered Mike. 'I'd not make an engineering job of it, as I haven't the experience.'

'Then pass it on to Mr Willerby, or else Ken Padgett. He's a biologist, and would take it in his stride.'

At this stage, it might be as well to describe the forces

at the disposal of Mr Willerby in his struggle to educate seventy-eight boys between the ages of eight and thirteen. In all, there were five assistant masters and one mistress for the lowest form. The most important teacher there, and this included Mr Willerby himself, was his second in command, Mr Anthony Coleridge. Old Willerby had no system whatsoever: he roared his way through the term, clutching to his bosom innumerable pieces of paper, the right one never being to hand. He employed his time bellowing for this or that boy, and cleaving a path through groups of them, who in no way resented his passage. Mr Coleridge was constantly creating order out of chaos, only to find pandemonium breaking out again, as his superior mucked things up. A very nice nature and a far-reaching sense of humour were the two things which just managed to preserve his sanity. He was a confirmed bachelor of forty, dedicated to his job but often with a rather worried look on his thin face.

Next in importance were Mr Williams and Mr Padgett. Both were young gentlemen of athletic build, but there the similarity ended. Mr Williams was a magnificent games player, a gifted coach and a positive encyclopaedia of sporting information. His Christianity resembled that of his employer, and it is to be feared, that the cross which he expected everyone to bear consisted of two uprights and a horizontal bar halfway up them. In the staff room, he talked about games both earnestly and incessantly, and his colleagues were infinitely surprised, that he should be able to find both the time and the inclination to be a lady-killer. The girlfriends whom Hugh Williams collected were a source of envy to his colleagues and of speculation to the Common Entrance form, who ran a book on their chances. Miss Fenwick, the under-matron, was considered a rank outsider, for she supported every first-class county in turn except Yorkshire, which was thought to be very daring. It should be stressed, that Hugh Williams was a Yorkshireman, and that Wintergreen was well within the borders of that county. The previous term, however, the youthful bookies had done well, for the games master and the under-matron returned as man and wife. The betting was then altered to cover the estimated date of arrival of their progeny.

Mr Padgett was of an entirely different breed. Games were of secondary importance to him, though he could run the length of the field carrying both the rugger ball and the entire opposition three-quarter line if they didn't tackle him in the way that Mr Williams had taught them. He was immensely fit, and ran the Scouts. He climbed and he sailed; he walked all night over mountainous country. He went on expeditions to Spitzbergen, and spent his holidays in uncomfortable trawlers. There was nothing tough that he was not prepared to undertake, and he was absolutely bursting with enthusiasm for gargantuan outdoor activities. In the common room, his talk was of these hearty pursuits, and poor Hugh Williams, who could hardly move a step without a ball or club, racquet or bat in his hand, was rather shocked that such a fine figure of a man should squander his obvious talents in this way. With equal zest, Ken Padgett taught the lesser subjects, science and geography and history (especially battles). They were fortunate in having such a champion, or they would have been totally overshadowed by the Latin of the headmaster, the French of his senior assistant and the mathematics of Hugh Williams.

The English teacher was a floater, one of those curious masters who spends his time moving on from school to school without ever really settling down anywhere. Sometimes they move on because they are inefficient, sometimes because they never can get on with their colleagues and sometimes it is simply because they like a change. In Mr Turner's case, he had an end in view. He was collecting data on headmasters for a monumental work which he intended writing on his final exit from the happy hunting grounds of the Incorporated Association of Preparatory Schools.

A year at a school was usually sufficient for him to complete his studies, but Old Willerby was out of the general run of headmasters, so Ned Turner, or Topsy as he was invariably called, needed two years to do him full justice. Topsy was a small, elfin figure who, when not taking notes in a corner, enjoyed retailing the scandals which he had collected over the years during his wanderings from school to school. It was almost impossible to mention a single member of the Association about which he knew nothing. When not on duty, he would disappear, bearing a little attaché case. This case was always kept locked: The Common Entrance form had tested it times without number, and they had formed the opinion that it contained drugs – purple hearts being the pusher's stock in trade at that time.

The last full member of the teaching staff was Miss Florence Fellowes, music and lower forms. Owing to her ability to inject the maximum amount of agitation into any given situation, her nickname was Flip Flap. She seldom stopped talking, and her hobby was other people's business. It was sometimes difficult to know whether she was just being silly, or whether there was malice aforethought. For years she had been after Tony Coleridge, but he evaded her attentions with the greatest good humour and complete success.

They were a very good staff, all, except Mike, being both well qualified and adequately paid. The atmosphere in the staff room was excellent, Old Willerby having the knack of keeping them all happy, though Flip Flap Florence sometimes made it difficult for him. Matron and her assistant were regarded as full members of the staff, and the only person who never joined in their activities was the rather shadowy Mrs Willerby, whose negative approach to life was the only possible method of coping with two such flamboyant figures as her husband and Matron. In her quiet way, she was good at comforting those in distress, whether boys or parents, but she had the good sense to regard the staff as beyond her terms of reference.

Later that evening, in fact only a few moments after Matron had spoken to him, Mike was recounting the incident to the assembled company. The general feeling was that he had come out of it with great credit. Flip Flap gushed on and on, until Topsy's tales of very much more embarrassing questions from small boys in half a dozen preparatory schools of his acquaintance drove her blushing from the room.

'She'll tell old Willerby, you see if she doesn't,' said Tony Coleridge.

'Couldn't care less. I'll take notes on his reactions,' said the impenitent Topsy. 'That woman really is an ass. I'd far sooner be on a desert island with Matron.'

Since Stevenson's name had been mentioned, the subject of conversation was very soon turned to his own advantage by Hugh Williams.

'Stevenson,' he said, 'has everything, speed, guts and a real rugger sense. I shall play him in the first fifteen on Saturday.'

'Won't he get knocked about too much?' asked Mike. His grammar school ran teams from under twelve upwards, it was rare for a small boy to be taken out of his age group.

'Good heavens, no,' answered Hugh in surprise. 'He's darned tough, and the experience will do him good.'

'Let's see,' said Tony, 'we're playing Grantley Lodge, aren't we?'

'Yes. They're very small this year. Now if it had been Bewd Hall, that would have been another matter.'

'Aren't they the school who had that big fast bowler?'

'Yes,' continued Hugh. 'I thought he was a master at first. Luckily, I was umpiring his end, and I damped down his ardour by no-balling him three times in the first over.'

'But, Hugh,' continued Tony, 'he frightened young Anderson so much that he has taken one pace to the rear at each ball bowled at him ever since.'

'Yes. Anderson disappointed me; he has a yellow streak in him, I'm afraid.'

'He showed darned good sense,' chipped in Ken Padgett, who had been doing interesting things to an anorak in the corner, and had so far kept remarkably quiet.

'Now coming from you, that's rich,' said Hugh, turning on him. 'You put yourself into needless danger all the ruddy time.'

'Ah, but if it really threatens, I keep out of it – or I should have been killed years ago.'

'To return to Bewd Hall,' said Tony, 'that bowler of theirs was as daft as a brush. I wonder if they got him in anywhere.'

'Why, yes,' said Hugh, 'he's passed the Common Entrance at last. Gone to Elmet, I think.'

Elmet was their nearest town, whose ancient public school was an unfailing last resort. Boys who seemed quite incapable of reaching any other public school in the land could generally get dumped there.

'I wonder what their GCE results are like,' queried Topsy. 'Every school I've ever been to has used Elmet as a kind of slag heap.'

'Their rugger's damned good, and that's what counts.'

It can be guessed who said that, and he continued:

'To return to Grantley Lodge, they've still got a goodish back row. Now you'll be refereeing, Ken, and I can rely on you. Pull them up for offside if they look like killing young Stevenson. A couple of penalties early on would do the trick.'

'I'm a humane man, Hugh. You can rely on me.'

'Given a fair chance, Stevenson will get the threes moving. He sends the ball out like a bullet.'

13

'A pity he can't spell better,' said Mike. 'That would be more use for him in life, wouldn't it?'

'Don't you believe it. Any smart Alec can spell, even you, Ken, but a born scrum half is rare. I've never seen a youngster like him.'

'I hope he won't waste all his life clutching a ball to his bosom,' said Ken, to no one in particular.

'Waste his life. What the blazes do you mean?' asked Hugh indignantly. 'I'll bet you half a dollar that boy'll play rugger for England.'

'I can think of better ways of spending one's time than shoving a ball into a scrum, and getting kicked in the guts if your side happens to heel it.'

'Honestly, Ken, I sometimes despair of you. Playing rugger is far safer than hanging on to a precipice by the eyebrows – or shooting those rapids in a second-hand canoe,' uttered the outraged Hugh, recalling one of Ken's more intrepid adventures.

'It was a damned good canoe,' was Ken's only comment.

By this time, it was past nine o'clock, and a visit to the pub was proposed. Most evenings, a party went down for a pint and a game of shove ha'penny. Darts and dominoes were the most popular pub games in this part of Yorkshire, in fact shove ha'penny was almost unknown, but some long-forgotten assistant manager had introduced it to the village, and it had been played nightly at the Green Dragon ever since. There were five boards, polished with loving care by the landlord, Jack Wright. There were halfpennies of graded weight, on each one of which someone spent many hours of highly illegal energy. Some players had their own sets, others relied on those provided by the establishment, but all of them slid so easily over the polished wood that great delicacy of touch was required. The lightweights had been rubbed away on one side until they were wafer-thin, and would bounce back up to an inch if they struck a heavier coin. The heavyweights, however, would follow through, scattering everything that was within their path. Hugh Williams played with astonishing skill, as one would expect, and it was seldom that anyone in the village beat him. Many of the others, however, were no mean performers, and rivalry was keen. Mike, a complete novice, was learning fast. The board in the staff room had been used for assiduous practice, and already he could beat Flip Flap, whose constant rush of words to the mouth was even more distracting to her than it was to her opponents.

'Who's on duty?' asked Hugh, as he polished his treasured coins. 'I was last night, so it can't be me.'

'I am really,' answered Tony, 'but Old Willerby's relieved me. He wants to stir things up tonight.'

'What on earth for?' asked Mike.

'Oh, he thinks it's time for someone to be beaten, so he causes a riot – and then quells it with his stick. I am always warned off when he's on the warpath.'

At this moment, Willerby himself marched in, wielding an unpleasant-looking weapon, in the form of a long and pliant cane.

'Good, evening,' he shouted. 'What have you people been doing to Flip Flap? She's been weeping on my shoulder.'

'She took exception to one of my stories, and a true one too,' owned up Topsy. 'She left the room in a cloud of disapproval.'

'She'll always be a foolish virgin, I think. One of these days I shall be stirring her up. Oh, Mike,' continued Old Willerby, 'you haven't met Attila yet, have you?'

'Attila, sir?'

'Yes, my cane – the Scourge of God. It's done yeoman service, I can tell you.'

As a matter of fact, it hadn't, for Old Willerby had worn out innumerable Attilas during his long career. When an ageing retainer became too tatty, it was cast into the fire.

Phoenix-like, another rose, as if from the ashes. This Attila was a comparative newcomer, obtained from the blind school in Elmet some months before. It was kept in a cupboard until the sacrificial consigning to the flames of its predecessor – and in its first week of office wrought havoc amongst the Common Entrance form.

'How interesting,' was the only comment that Mike could produce.

Old Willerby dealt the table a friendly whack, which was so loud that it must have given the warning signal to many of his flock.

'You might apologise to Flip Flap,' he said to Topsy. 'You needn't be too profuse, you know. She'll be chattering nineteen to the dozen, and won't listen to you.'

'Certainly, Headmaster, it's the gesture which counts,' said Topsy, as Attila and its owner charged out of the staff room, both thirsting for instant action.

When the door shut, Topsy announced that he would not be going down to the pub with them. Quite apart from his interview with Flip Flap, he wished to take notes on the stirring-up process. It was therefore a quartet which sallied forth into the night – Tony and Ken, Hugh and Mike.

2

The Willerby family had lived at Wintergreen Hall for several hundred years, and the green dragon on the inn sign was a small portion of their elaborate coat of arms. This same green dragon appeared upon the caps and blazers, notepaper and exercise books of the very large family which old Walter Willerby, the present headmaster's father, had decided to collect together at the turn of the century. Whilst remaining Lord of the Manor of Wintergreen, he had found ample time to run his school. Young Willerby, as he then was, was born and bred there and, in the fullness of time, he took over from his father.

The Hall stood at one end of the village of Wintergreen, guarding its approach from the north. It was originally a fortified manor house, and later additions augmented its charm. An ancient gatehouse led into an enclosed quadrangle. On either side was a range of lesser buildings, whilst the main house faced the gateway. In the centre of the quadrangle was a lawn which had been the pride of the Willerbys for many generations. It was the only part of the house and grounds which the boys were never allowed to desecrate. One foot upon the sacred turf, and Attila was called upon to deal with the intrusion. It was about the size of a tennis court, but even Hugh had never dared to suggest that it might be used for that purpose. He did not so much as set foot upon its weedless expanse, for Old Willerby kept a loaded shotgun in his bedroom, and Old Willerby's bedroom window looked out upon the quadrangle. He never had discharged it

17

at a member of his staff, but there could always be a first time.

The four drinkers went out of the front door, walked round the lawn and passed through the archway. There were two portcullises, one at each end of the passageway. These were in good working order, and, on one side of the guardroom door, there were marks in the stone where Willerby retainers, in days gone by, had sharpened, their swords. It is seldom that a school possesses on the premises such aids to the study of ancient history.

'Did you know,' asked Ken, as they emerged, 'that a Willerby led his bowmen beneath this archway on their way to Agincourt?'

'I bet he stirred them up if they didn't shoot straight,' was Mike's comment.

'He probably had one of those chain things, with a ball on the end,' said Hugh. 'I wonder if that too was called Attila.'

'He was certainly very successful,' continued Ken. 'The family income was doubled by the ransom money which he collected.'

The party strolled to the end of the village. On their right, and opposite the church, was the Green Dragon. Its hospitable doors, front during opening hours and back at other times of the day and night, stood open to the public. It was a long, low building, which had certainly been standing since the late sixteenth century. To prove this, there was an extremely vulgar message scratched on a pane of glass in the public bar. Dated 1588, it questioned the legitimacy of the Duke of Medina Sidonia, and applauded the exploits of Sir Francis Drake, had it been scribbled on the walls of the Wintergreen lavatories, Old Willerby would have had a field day, but great antiquity lent respectability to the scribble. It was now rated high up the list of historical graffiti, and from many countries learned gentlemen came to inspect it. Quite apart from the actual value of the writing, it was one of the few remaining panes of sixteenth-century glass to be found on licensed premises.

'Evening all,' said Hugh, eagerly looking round to see if there were any opponents worthy of his mettle.

'Four pints of bitter,' said Tony to the landlord, who found time to take the mug from his own mouth in order to attend to their wants.

'Now there's a lovely pint of beer,' he said, as he passed the first pint over.

It certainly was extremely clear, and Jack Wright was not the kind of fellow to be silent about it. It is to be feared that Jack would long ago have sampled his wares to the point of extinction, had not his wife rationed him severely. He was a cheerful Yorkshireman who had taken over the pub on demobilisation in 1945, and had grown in girth and joviality ever since. He had a daughter and two sons, both of whom had been at the school as day boys. Old Willerby was always prepared to take in the local lads at a reasonable fee, but most of them went to the village school, where it was considered that they would not get ideas above their station. Jack, however, thought himself and his family to be the equal of the best in the land, and he could well afford the fees.

'Thirsty work looking after t'little baskets?' he asked, as four faces sank beneath the rims of the tankards.

'Better now that both yours have left us,' answered Tony.

'You wait while my grandson comes along,' continued Jack, whose daughter had recently produced a fine future Wintergreener.

'What about a game, Jack?' asked Hugh, seeing that there were no village experts in the bar anxious to take him on.

'OK, Ugh. Just a short one – one 'orse, one in a bed.'

There are some who are unfortunate enough to pass through life without ever playing a game of shove ha'penny, and some explanation is required for their benefit. The

board has ten lines drawn across it, making nine compart-
ments, or beds, in which the coins must come to rest.
Normally, the game goes on until one player has filled up
all nine beds three times, the score being chalked up in
spaces provided at the side of the board when each player
has finished his turn. Each game is called a horse, the
reason being lost in antiquity, and the normal match is best
of three horses. Jack was cutting down the contest very
considerably to a short, sharp five minutes, which was about
as long as his thirstier clients could wait before their glasses
needed replenishing.

Jack produced a penny, and asked Hugh to call. With
strangers he invariably won the toss, for he had two pennies,
one double-headed and the other double-tailed. He was
able to swap them over most skilfully, and had no hesitation
in employing these doubtful tactics on anyone foolish enough
to call before the coin was in the air. Even those in the
know were sometimes caught out, as Hugh was this time.

'Heads,' he called out absentmindedly, and then made
a wild but abortive snatch at Jack's hand.

'Bad luck, it's tails,' said Jack without looking. 'I'll go
first, of course.'

'Oh, blast you, Jack,' said Hugh. 'I never could stand
dishonesty.'

'Who are you calling dishonest? You'd play any trick to
win. Gamesmanship, you call it. It's only dishonest if someone
catches you out – which aren't often.'

Jack played his five coins with great deliberation, and
succeeded, in filling the end bed. This one is always tricky,
and he was well content.

'Ow's that for a start?' he began, and managed to go on
talking all the time that Hugh was playing, just in case he
could put him off. The plan did not work.

'I don't need to concentrate, thank God,' said Hugh, as
he chalked up three beds.

Jack's second was also a good one, and he filled three beds too. One of them was a little close, for the coin has to be well clear of the lines, but Jack chalked it in quickly before a post-mortem could be organised.

'Hey, wait a minute. That's never in,' was all that Hugh could say before Jack had removed the coins.

'Course it was. Get on with your turn; I 'aven't got all night.'

Hugh promptly filled another two, then Jack did the same, but he gave one away. If a coin stops in a bed which is already filled, and one's opponent needs it, the point is chalked up to him. It goes without saying that Jack conceded the point with a show of reluctance. This left each of them with three more beds to fill, and it was Hugh's turn. He promptly filled in two of them, and suggested that Jack might give him the game.

'I'm bound to win,' he said, 'and you're needed behind the bar.'

'Don't you believe it,' countered Jack, and filled one more bed. It would have been two if a neutral observer had not been called in to decide whether it was in or not. The man was truthful rather than tactful, for it is always as well to keep in with mine host.

'You'll not get a drink out of hours this side of Christmas,' said Jack, but he accepted his decision.

Hugh had now only the end bed to fill, but even the most gifted can have an off day, and he gave Jack one more chance to win. With his second coin Jack filled the nearer one, and now the filling of the eighth bed remained between him and a notable victory.

'Just you watch this one,' he said, as he struck his heaviest coin. It stopped a tiny fraction short.

'That's in, isn't it?'

'No, it darned well isn't, and you know it,' said Hugh, but he was visibly shaken.

21

Jack had now to give the coin the most delicate of touches, a faint graze on one side to edge it in. His fourth shot was not hard enough, and stopped short. With great skill, Jack steered his last coin between obstructions, but it jumped and part of it rested on top of the heavy coin, now well and truly in the eighth bed.

'Right, Ogh, I win,' he said, making a move to collect up the coins.

'Oh no, you don't,' said Hugh. 'That doesn't count, they're copulating.'

The term may not be universal, but the rule is. Then one coin is on top of another, neither coin can be counted.

'What? Oh, yes, so they are,' said Jack, as if he hadn't noticed.

Hugh made short work of it his next turn, and even Jack had to admit defeat. He retired behind the bar, and was gracious enough to send a pint across to his conqueror. The quartet then played a noisy foursome, Mike being such a handicap to Hugh that their opponents won quite comfortably.

''Ow's old 'Oratia?' asked Jack during a lull. 'The old girl's a wonder. She's 'ardly changed since t'war.'

'Why, did you know her then?' asked Mike.

'I should think I did. She nearly married my skipper. She'd 'ave given 'im 'ell if she 'ad.'

'What? Matron nearly married? I don't believe it.'

'Well, she was engaged. I 'eard 'er propose myself.'

'What went wrong?'

'T'Japs spoilt it for them,' said Jack, and he said it in a tone which seemed to indicate that he did not wish to elaborate.

'Tell Mike about how you won the war, Jack,' said Ken. 'He hasn't heard, how you got that thing.'

He pointed towards a medal pinned, up behind the bar, quite obviously a trophy of some value to Jack.

'I'd 'ave you know, young man, that "that thing" means a lot to me. I 'ad to suffer to get it.'

'What did you do?' asked Mike dutifully. 'Sink an enemy battleship or rescue the Admiral?'

'Well, actually I didn't do nowt. We drew lots for it.'

'Then how did you suffer?'

'I was kissed twice by a bloody little Frenchman before he'd give it me. In front of whole ship's company too.'

'How did you manage to earn a French decoration?' asked Mike.

'It was after the Madagascar campaign. Nineteen-forty-two, it was,' continued Jack in his choicest Yorkshire accent.

'But weren't we fighting the French there?'

'We were – and then again we weren't. Our job was to capture an island, called Maquemique. It was owned by the Vichy French, but the inhabitants were one big fifth column. I got me medal from the Gaullist lot.'

'And what is the medal?'

'It's the "Croicks Makalache". The skipper and another officer got one too.'

'*Croix*, not Croicks,' muttered Tony, the schoolmaster in him coming to the fore.

'Very well, then "*croix*" if you like – damned silly language, French, anyway. We hurtled over the reef, and landed the black pongos. Combined operation, you know.'

'Seems an odd sort of ship. What was she – a canoe?'

'No, an old river gunboat, HMS *Beetle*. A cyclone got her in the end. Skipper was a Polish count, a real gent.'

'And he's the chap who was engaged to Matron?' continued Mike.

'Yes, a grand lad. I never took much to naval officers, somehow, but *Beetle* collected all t'good'uns in t'Royal Navy.'

'You must tell us more about them some other time,' said Tony. 'I must take the lads back, or there'll be trouble.'

'Ay, there will. T'Squire will be shutting you out.'

To boys and staff, he was Old Willerby, or O.W. for short, but to the villagers he was still 't' Squire'. On one occasion, he had lowered a portcullis just to teach his staff not to stay out all night on the tiles, and refused to pull it up again until Matron had interceded on their behalf. She said that the boys would suffer if the staff slept all night in the road.

With the approach of Saturday's match, excitement mounted rapidly. The team was eventually picked by Hugh, but not before a whole heap of conflicting advice had been given by his colleagues and ignored by him, and Stevenson's name appeared amongst the immortals. The first sign of a cloud, no bigger than a man's hand, appeared on the very morning of the match.

'Please, sir,' said Macpherson, one of the Common Entrance form, 'do you think we shall win?'

No preparatory school match has ever been played without that question being asked several dozen times before the game. However bleak their chances might be, no master would be tactless enough to say 'no', and, being optimists anyway, small boys always go onto the field of battle full of hope.

'Oh, we stand a good chance,' answered Hugh. 'I don't think that Grantley Lodge are all that good.'

'But, sir, Mr Willerby says we're playing Bewd Hall.'

'No, Grantley Lodge, Macpherson. You've got it wrong, We don't play Bewd Hall until after half-term.'

All the same, he was a little shaken, and before lunch he checked it up with Old Willerby. After looking through a whole host of papers on his desk, none of which seemed to have any bearing on rugger or anything else, the latter was unable to say whether it was Grantley Lodge or Bewd Hall, but it definitely wasn't St Oswald's this Saturday. Hugh hastily detailed the second team scrum half, a stolid youth of great toughness but little talent, to stand by in case Bewd Hall came. There was some tension before the visitors arrived, and the Common Entrance form fixed the odds at five to four, in marbles, on Grantley Lodge.

At two o'clock precisely, three cars drove through the gateway – it was the St Oswald's team.

The headmaster of St Oswald's stepped out first, and noticed at once that something was amiss. He was a youngish man who relied, without much success, on what he considered to be his excellent memory.

'What's wrong?' he asked, as he shook hands with Old Willerby. 'We are playing you, aren't we?'

'No,' answered O.W.

'But we fixed it up after the cricket last term. When we got rained off. Don't you remember?'

'No,' said O.W.

'It didn't rain either time we played you, and we won both times,' said Hugh, possibly rather tactlessly.

'Oh dear, so you did,' acknowledged the head of St Oswald's. 'It must have been Bewd Hall. Do you mind if I give them a ring and tell them that we shall be arriving late?'

'There you are,' said Hugh, 'if Bewd Hall are entertaining St Oswald's, Grantley Lodge are coming here.'

After Old Willerby had led off his opposite number to telephone, a coach arrived at the gatehouse – it contained the Bewd Hall team.

'Oh, my God,' said Hugh. 'Now we've got two lots of opponents. What on earth can we do?'

'Let down the portcullis,' answered Ken. 'They aren't in yet.'

Before the parley had got under way, and explanations could be given, yet another coachload of small boys arrived – this time it was the Grantley Lodge first-fifteen, plus registered spectators.

25

'How many different schools do we play?' asked Mike. 'If they all show up, the only hope is to turn it into a cross-country race, ten from each team to count.'

Fortunately, the stream of visitors now dried up, and a conference was held. There were four teams, and, whilst the blame for the mix-up could not be correctly apportioned in one sitting, it was agreed that Grantley Lodge should pair off with Wintergreen and Bewd Hall should take on St Oswald's. This was, in point of fact, the original arrangement, and the members of the conference passed the resolution, *nem. con.* that in future a rather less casual approach to fixtures should be adopted by those responsible for the present difficulty.

The next problem to be decided was which schools should have the honour of playing on the first game pitch. Wintergreen generously volunteered to put St Oswald's and Bewd Hall there, but Grantley Lodge objected strongly. The second game pitch was an irregular quadrilateral, and had a series of minor Alps in the centre; there was, moreover, a large horse chestnut tree in one corner. Grantley Lodge maintained, correctly, that Wintergreen's knowledge of the terrain was worth ten points at least to them, whilst the peculiarities of the pitch would be equally unknown to Bewd Hall and St Oswald's. They insisted on the better field, much to the mortification of the head of St Oswald's and the Bewd Hall games master, who got into a huddle in a quiet corner and had a talk.

'What about going on to Bewd Hall?' said Mr Arnold, of St Oswald's.

'It wouldn't be popular with my head,' answered Mr Innes, of Bewd Hall. 'He'd never lay on a team tea at such short notice. We could get over to St Oswald's in three-quarters of an hour.'

'Same trouble there. I'd have all the domestic staff leaving in a body. We'd better stay here and play.'

'Well, what sort of a meal will we get, anything at all?'

'Oh, yes. With Old Willerby the unexpected often happens. They're used to major crises here, and the Wintergreen team teas are damned good. We'll stay.'

A further problem then arose. Who was to referee the Bewd Hall–St Oswald's game? It had to be a Wintergreen master, for neither Mr Arnold nor Mr Innes was prepared to do the job in his braces. The question was, which Wintergreen master? The real rugger players were Hugh and Ken, though all of the men could take a game at a pinch. Hugh insisted on watching his own team from the touchline, and Ken was refereeing the other match, so they were ruled out. Topsy was not on parade, having been spotted on his way out carrying his little attaché case shortly after lunch.

'Now then, Mike,' said Tony, 'either I do the refereeing and you help to collect enough eggs for the extra team tea, or vice versa.'

'I'll go and change,' said Mike very quickly. 'I can always hide behind the chestnut tree if things get out of hand on the field of battle, but I don't fancy helping Matron to lay three dozen eggs.'

Old Willerby heard this – he had also seen the headmaster of Grantley Lodge turn in at the gatehouse in a large Jag. He didn't relish the idea of standing on the touchline listening to his only two subjects of conversation: the hard times which he was going through and the way his team was being robbed of tries by bad luck, the referee and the hand of God.

'You've hardly the experience, Mike,' said O.W. 'You go and fix up the visitors' changing accommodation, and I'll referee the match.'

'Are you sure you can manage, sir?' asked Mike.

'Of course I can. I was playing rugger before any of you were born.'

27

'That's really what I mean, sir. It won't be too much for you?'

'Too much – don't be silly. I'll be ready in five minutes.'

He stomped off to change, and Mike had the unenviable task of fitting forty-five boys into a changing–room designed for roughly half that number. He directed operations from outside, or some of them would have had to strip in the passage.

Eventually, the three teams were ready, Bewd Hall in yellow and green, St Oswald's in brown and white and Grantley Lodge in plain blue. They surged down onto the fields, where the two referees, the Wintergreen team and quite an assorted crowd of spectators was already waiting. There they must be left for a moment, whilst the feverish attempts to produce a team tea up to the Wintergreen standard are chronicled.

It would be an exaggeration to say that food is the most important thing in a preparatory school match, but it cannot be denied that a really good tea makes up for a smashing defeat, an indifferent referee or the type of injury which is likely to be inflicted in the rough and tumble of an inter-school rugger match. Many an incipient concussion has been cured by the thought that only instant recovery will avert the catastrophic loss of a darned good meal. Some schools do the bare minimum, others produce something which a chap can remember for weeks. Of the four schools present, Wintergreen was undoubtedly at the top of the league. There were always lashings of just the right food: luscious cakes for all and mixed grill and chips for the boys. Grantley Lodge tried to make up for lack of calories by serving up rather a poor meal with the style of a five-star hotel or the country home of a belted earl. A butler was much in evidence, but knowledgeable visitors did not see fit to prepare for the meal by earlier abstinence. Bewd Hall produced masses of very poor food, great doorsteps of bread and not much margarine, rock cakes resembling rock rather than cake and large but mainly inedible sausages for the boys. At St Oswald's, you never knew quite what would happen. Sometimes, Mr Arnold's domestic staff produced a spread almost up to Wintergreen standard, at others the fare was more meagre than a Grantley Lodge repast and more unappetising than anything which Bewd Hall supplied. The housekeeper apparently drew items out of a hat and shared them impartially between adults and boys. The finest China tea, which tasted to them of dirty water, would be given to the boys: a witches' brew, already mixed with milk and sugar, would be given to visiting parents out of a chipped enamel pot. It was said that in this liquid the spoons, as well as tea leaves and foreign matter, would float around quite happily.

Tea, then, was definitely important, and the efficient Tony was a very busy man that afternoon. Before the first blast of the first whistle, he had spread the shattering news that twice the number of boys and three times the number of adults would be expecting to partake of a Wintergreen tea. Mrs Willerby was outwardly calm, and merely asked Tony to pass on the information to Matron. She had seen quite enough of the cook that day already, and was not going to put herself out if her fool of a husband had collected at least fifty guests in excess of the normal quota for a match–day tea.

'If there's any trouble, let me know,' she said vaguely, and Tony thought to himself that if she couldn't see trouble now she never would.

Matron's attitude was entirely different. In a moment, she had grasped, the full implication of the situation, and was weighing up the best methods of enforcing that every man, and woman too, should do his or her duty.

'We must make an engineering job of this,' she said. 'Collect up Pat Williams, and report to the kitchen.'

Now Pat Williams was resting, as any young lady in her

condition is entitled to do, but she obeyed the summons with the utmost despatch. Not only was she afraid of Matron, but also she felt that the honour of Wintergreen was at stake. Her husband was coping on the field of battle, and she must see to a suitable reception for the returning warriors. She sprang from her couch, to follow close on Tony's heels as he sped towards the kitchen. There, Matron was already rallying the domestic forces, Mrs Emmerson, the cook, and two underlings. She turned to Tony as he entered, and asked:

'How many hangers-on have they brought?'

'Boys or adults, Matron?'

'Boys first. They're more important.'

'Four touch-judges and seven spectators from Grantley Lodge. We needn't feed them, you know.'

'Nonsense. Of course, we must. The poor little devils will be half–starved; they don't get enough to eat at that place.'

'Very well, Matron. That's sixty players and eleven others – seventy-one in all.'

'Oh, my God,' said Mrs Emmerson, and she meant it.

'Pipe down,' said Matron. 'They'll fit into the dining-room nicely. Now, Mr Coleridge, what about the adults?'

'I'll go and count, if you like, but my estimate is between thirty and forty.'

'Call it forty,' said Matron.

'Oh, my God,' said Mrs Emmerson even more fervently.

'Can't you say something more helpful?' asked Matron, turning on her. 'It's a case of all hands to the pumps – but you can pray quietly to yourself.'

'Now what exactly are we short of?' asked Tony.

'Everything,' said Mrs Emmerson.

'Nonsense,' said Matron. 'For a start, we've tea and milk and sugar, bread and butter and jam.'

This roused Mrs Emmerson to something more than monosyllables, and she came in with a telling antiphon.

'Ay, but there's cakes and ham and eggs, tomatoes and sausages...'

Before the list could be extended indefinitely, Tony broke in.

'But we can get all these at the village shop, can't we?'

'Not cakes,' said Mrs Emmerson lugubriously, but perhaps with a touch of triumph. 'I make them all myself.'

'And very good they are, but we'll have to supplement what you've already made with something inferior. There's no time to go into Elmet, so the choice is limited,' said Tony.

'A little hard tack will do no harm. The stores have some excellent biscuits.'

'Yes, Matron. Tap them, and the weevils come out most satisfactorily. Give me a list, and I'll see what I can do.'

'Aye, aye,' said Matron, writing down as Mrs Emmerson started, to dictate. 'We'll make an engineering job of this yet.'

As she was speaking, Flip Flap twittered in.

'Oh, Tony,' she said, 'isn't it awful? What are we to do? There won't be a real tea, I'm sure there won't, and...'

'Stop wringing your hands, and get busy with the butter knife,' said Matron, who did not suffer her very gladly.

Flip Flap, however, was in full cry, and heeded not the executive command.

'Oh dear, we'll never be ready for all this crowd. And there isn't sufficient food to go round. I'll pop into Elmet by bus and get some cakes.'

'Oh no, you won't. You'd have to eat them all yourself, as you wouldn't be back in time. Stop dithering – we've no time for idle gossip, or we'll never be shipshape and Bristol fashion.'

Matron thrust the handle of a knife into her hand, and then she and Mrs Emmerson completed Tony's list.

'Be back in twenty minutes, Mr Coleridge,' she called out. 'Full ahead both.'

31

'Both what, Matron?' asked Flip Flap.

'Both engines, Miss Fellowes, both engines. It means that he has to move with speed.'

'I can't understand what you're saying half the time,' said Flip Flap plaintively. 'I try to teach the boys good English, and you employ a sort of naval jargon.'

Matron did not bother to reply, but merely swelled from the bust upwards, a manoeuvre which was most effective in quelling both senior officers and Wrens during her days of active service. She then attacked the bread herself with ferocity, thereby setting the ratings such a magnificent example that the kitchen hummed with industry. Tony returned with the necessary extra victuals in plenty of time. He then left the five ladies at it, knowing quite well that, with Matron at the helm, all would be ready at the appointed time. He wanted to find out what was happening down on the playing fields, for he felt that O.W. could have snarled things up extensively by this time, and that his services might be required to straighten out what Matron was apt to call, when the boys were nominally out of hearing, 'a proper nest of bastards', a term frequently employed in the Navy when things have gone wrong.

A new chapter is clearly required, for much had happened, was happening and was going to happen on the two fields of battle. It should be mentioned at this point that these matches took place in the good old days when three, not five points, were awarded for a try. The result of one match, indeed, would have been different had it been played these enlightened days. Moreover, yards and not metres were used for measuring, so the old-fashioned sensible 'twenty-five' takes the place of that miserable, modern 'twenty-two'.

3

It was just on half-time when Tony arrived, and much of interest had been crowded into that short first half. A prep school rugger match is only twenty-five minutes each way, but none of the spectators could complain that he hadn't had his money's worth. The home team and Grantley Lodge had played good rugger, though interruptions from the other game did tend to throw them occasionally off their stride. The abnormalities of the pitch and the vagaries of the referee, however, made sound orthodox play impossible for St Oswald's and Bewd Hall. Not that sound orthodox play was usually encountered at either school. Bewd Hall relied on sheer brute force, having always at least one gigantic champion on whom, like the Philistines, they relied exclusively. St Oswald's, on the other hand, had the knack of breeding Davids, for whom sound orthodox play would be both unprofitable and deadly dull. They didn't actually cheat intentionally, but they had a refreshingly free interpretation of the rules of the game – which could cause acute distress to the opposition. When they won the toss, and their captain said – 'We'll defend the tree,' he had already seen that the obstruction could be treated as a valuable ally.

The toss-up itself was quite spectacular, for Old Willerby had taken up a position on a hillock, and summoned the rival captains in stentorian tones. He towered above them both, the current Bewd Hall Goliath being far too dumb to act as captain. Like the referee in a title fight, he cautioned them on what they must, and must not, do. Quite clearly, he was going to enjoy himself hugely. After delivering his oration, which everyone within a quarter of a mile could hear quite distinctly, he made the two captains shake hands, and indicated that he was ready for their teams to take up action stations.

When the St Oswald's captain returned to his men, he showed that he had made full use of his time on the hilltop. Like Alexander the Great, he had surveyed the battlefield, and, like Alexander the Great, he had learnt much from his recce.

'There's plenty of dead ground,' he said to his companions, 'but we'll have to entice the old boy into a valley before we can exploit the situation to our advantage.'

The normal captain of a prep school fifteen neither talks nor thinks like this, but St Oswald's prided itself on producing boys of an original turn of mind.

All this took time, and the other match was well under way before Old Willerby's game had started. A Grantley Lodge wing three-quarter was away on his own, with no one to stop him, when O.W. was still adjusting his watch. He looked up in horror, saw that his school was going to be three points down and gave an almighty blast on his whistle. This had the desired effect of setting his own game in motion, and preventing Grantley Lodge from scoring a certain try. Their wing man pulled up, and by the time that he had discovered that the summons was not for him, the Wintergreen defence had gathered sufficient strength to repel boarders. Old Willerby was well satisfied, and was then able to give the match which he was controlling his undivided attention.

Bewd Hall kicked off. With the full weight of Goliath's eleven stone behind it, the ball soared upwards in the general direction of the tree. It was, in the long run, disastrous for Bewd Hall that the St Oswald's full back muffed it, and a set scrum was ordered well inside the St

Oswald's twenty-five. There was hearty applause from the Bewd Hall supporters, and Goliath was quite convinced that from then onwards the only thing to do was to kick the ball as hard as he could on the many occasions that his team handed it to him. In this way, an irresistible force permanently neutralised itself, and the odds against a St Oswald's victory shortened considerably.

The next thing to be done was to reduce Goliath's mobility, for he was capable of following up his kicks almost at the speed of sound. It was here that the tree came to the aid of St Oswald's. After a quick heel, unsound tactics when on the defence the purist might say, the St Oswald's backs got the ball. They made little effort to advance, but whipped it along the three-quarter line towards the horse chestnut. Goliath followed it, the earth shaking as he thundered by. It was unfortunate for him that the wing man dodged behind the tree at his approach, for he tackled it with vigour and was never quite the same after the encounter. He was too heavy to carry off, and anyway, the Bewd Hall boys were remarkably tough. He soon recovered sufficiently to stand upright, so the game proceeded according to the St Oswald's plan.

Then from the other game came a shrill cheer, harsh as the cutting edge of a saw. It proclaimed that the home team had scored, and a minute figure, more boots than anything else, picked himself and the ball up from beneath the posts. The day was made for Stevenson, and future England selectors, though they did not know it, were one step nearer filling the scrum half position in fifteen years' time. Four female Stevensons on the touchline were suitably impressed, and Mike thought how unbearable Hugh Williams was going to be now that his young protégé had made the grade. An excellent kick increased the Wintergreen lead, much to the chagrin of the headmaster of Grantley Lodge. Turning to Mike, who was standing next to him, he complained:

'Offside by a mile. What a referee! Don't you agree?'

'Perhaps the sun got in his eyes,' was all that Mike could think of saying, which wasn't very clever, as it was just beginning to rain.

It was just beginning to rain, and Old Willerby was wearing glasses. The fact did not escape the St Oswald's team, and their interpretation of the rules became considerably more free in consequence. A couple of quick penalties against them warned them that the referee's vision was not entirely obscured, so they calmed down a little. After the second infringement, O.W. pulled the culprit to one side, and whispered noisily:

'I used to try that one on when your father was still in nappies.'

His father, on the far touchline, took exception to this remark, but his mouth was kept so full of hot buttered crumpet at tea that he was never able to register a coherent complaint.

The only other score on either game before half-time was due to the perspicacity of the St Oswald's captain. Choosing his spot well, he stooped down, ostensibly to tie up his bootlace, and disappeared from view. The ball eventually came within his reach, whereupon he seized it and was off like a snipe before anyone realised that he was there. His unexpected appearance amongst the Philistines surprised them so much that he was able to dart across their line before any of them could take action. After the conversion had failed, Bewd Hall kicked off again, this time towards the left or treeless side. It was another mighty effort, and found touch on the St Oswald's twenty-five.

Now it so happened that the two fields had a common touchline, and also that a Wintergreen defender had found touch at precisely the same spot. So intent were the linesmen on their job that they met head on, and fell together upon the greensward. It is seldom that one game has to be stopped so that a linesman can receive medical attention; that two linesmen from two separate games should be tended at the same time on the same touchline is surely unique. Both the St Oswald's and the Grantley Lodge touch judges received black eyes, and the latter's headmaster felt even more strongly than usual that God was not on his side.

There was one other feature of the St Oswald's–Bewd Hall match which should be mentioned, though its full implications were not foreseen, and the crowning catastrophe of the game did not take place until the very end of the match. Goliath's constant kicks ahead, which have already been mentioned, resulted in trouble which would not normally affect an inter–school rugger match. The pull of gravity ensures that a rugger ball, however high it is kicked, will invariably come down to earth somewhere – but not if there is a large horse chestnut tree on the field of play. Quite early, the balls began to roost there, a fact which was envisaged when Hugh Williams had brought down the school's entire stock of rugger balls. By the time that Old Willerby eventually blew his whistle for the changeover, there were no fewer than seven balls in the tree, so that from a distance it resembled an incipient rookery. At first, Old Willerby ordered a set scrum at its base, but he began to think, quite erroneously, that the balls were going up there of malice aforethought. After the third lodgement, he ordered a penalty against the offending side, so St Oswald's were able to relieve very serious pressure on four occasions purely because of the tree.

At half-time, when a rather smaller segment of orange than usual was being devoured by the players, O.W. calculated that the supply of balls would not last out. He therefore called upon the services of a good climber, and a horde of volunteers poured onto the field. Young Anderson, the farmer's son and an intrepid mountaineer, was pushed up into the foliage, and managed to retrieve five of the balls before his attentions wandered to the fabulous crop of conkers still in situ. The teams changed over, therefore, with two balls still in the tree, and for most of the second half the number remained constant, for Goliath was now kicking away from the timber which had ruined his every move.

Before the second half did start, Tony contacted his superior, who announced to the assembled company that there would be plenty of tea for all, a statement which brought forth prolonged cheering from everybody present. That his bellow stopped a very promising forward rush on the part of the Grantley Lodge pack, for their game had been under way for some minutes, was noted and adversely commented upon by the Grantley Lodge headmaster.

'He did it on purpose, I know he did,' he complained, but it was Hugh to whom he addressed this remark, and it fell on stony ground.

'We had the situation well under control,' he said. 'We'd have halted you, gained possession and gone into the attack, so actually the stoppage favoured you.'

Both games continued fiercely for the next quarter of an hour, with no further score, but at last the Grantley Lodge persistence was rewarded. Their stylish wing man got away, and there was no clarion call from O.W. to stop his triumphant progress. He scored, amidst polite clapping from the Wintergreen supporters and a gallant imitation of the Wintergreen roar from the seven official spectators whom Grantley Lodge had brought with them.

The attempt to convert was really a brilliant effort. From a long way out, their kicker sent the ball soaring upwards towards the posts. It hit the cross bar and bounced back, thereby causing a cheer from two or three ill–bred Wintergreeners, hastily hushed up by the staff. From the headmaster of Grantley Lodge's remarks, one would have thought that the Almighty had raised the cross bar three

inches on purpose, and then dropped it back into place
when it had done its fell work. Another five minutes of
ding-dong struggle, and the final whistle blew.

'A very good game,' conceded the defeated headmaster,
'but we ought to have won.'

'Oh, I don't know about that,' said Hugh. 'I felt that we
had much more of the ball.'

If Wintergreen had won by the most fortunate of flukes,
Hugh would have been the last to admit it.

And now, all eyes were fixed upon the Homeric struggle
on the other field. In the dying minutes of the game, St
Oswald's were pressing. Their backs to the line, Bewd Hall
were defending dourly. At last, their Goliath got the ball,
and kicked it with a despairing force – slap into the branches
of the forbidden tree. This time, however, it did not stick
there. Indeed the reverse might be said to have happened,
for there was a positive shower of rugger balls. The newcomer,
ricocheting from one to the other, dislodged both balls
which were already resident there. Goliath pounced upon
the nearest one, and became the spearhead of a Bewd Hall
phalanx, which ploughed its way through the St Oswald's
ranks. They forced a path first to the line, then on into
enemy territory, eventually finishing over the line in a neat
heap. Fourteen of the St Oswald's team buzzed around
them like angry bees, but all to no avail. O.W. blew his
whistle – Bewd Hall had drawn level.

But had they? There are fifteen in a team, and only
fourteen St Oswald's stalwarts had struggled unavailingly in
the great retreat. Where was the odd man, and why had
he so cravenly refused to fight? It was their redoubtable
captain too, and surely he could not be hiding his head in
shame in some undulation upon the field of battle.

As a matter of fact, he wasn't. Unseen by all but a couple
of Bewd Hall defenders, he had pounced on another of
the descending shower of balls, dodging smartly behind the

tree. During Bewd Hall's all-conquering advance with the other ball, he had evaded those who sought to stop him, and dived across the line. He was now watching events with a slightly bewildered air, as were the enemy couple who had failed to arrest his progress.

'Hi, sir!' he shouted, 'I scored up here first. Doesn't my try count?'

Old Willerby looked round, and realised that the fellow might have a case.

'Come here, boy,' he shouted back, 'and bring that ball with you.'

He had the mistaken idea that he could establish the identity of the ball which had been in play, but on inspection the two of them were identical. The third ball was brought to him from where it had fallen, and to all intents and purposes the twins had become triplets. Here was a problem whose solution would require a whole bench of Solomons. Which try was to be allowed, or was there to be no score at all? The verdict, whatever O.W.'s decision, would be a talking point for years to come.

'Boys,' he announced after due deliberation, 'you have probably made history. For the first time ever, both sides have scored a try at one and the same time. Take the kicks.'

All but one kicker from each side retired behind their own goal lines, O.W. stopped in the middle of the field, his head moving slowly to and fro like an elderly tortoise in search of lettuce, and the linesmen, after some hesitation, each took up a position behind the opposition posts.

Bewd Hall converted, and St Oswald's did not. A gigantic kick by Goliath gained two points for Bewd Hall, whilst the St Oswald's captain, his only lack of success in that homeric struggle, failed miserably. This had no bearing on the result, but excitement was intense. With the score at six to St Oswald's and five to Bewd Hall, Old Willerby blew 'no side', well content with his prowess, and more than ready for a quick bath and the famous Wintergreen tea.

Tea was safely over, and the guests had long since departed. From their happy, even carefree, expressions it was impossible to guess who had won. Even the headmaster of Grantley Lodge, whose face at the end of the game had been as long as the bonnet of his glittering car, had departed with a smile on his face. He'd had a far better meal than he could ever hope to eat within his own walls, and the surfeit of crumpets had not yet begun to pain him. The black eyes of the linesmen were beginning to please their owners, and Goliath's collision with the tree was not even a painful memory, for he had quite forgotten why he was feeling somewhat bent. Both boys and masters at Wintergreen were elated, and one might think that Hugh Williams would have had nothing else to talk about but his own team's superb play and his headmaster's masterly handling of the other match.

Most unfortunately, this was not the case. It will be remembered that his wife had leapt from her bed straight into the fray, and that she had struggled valiantly over the provision of the tea. She, as much as anyone else, was surprised when intense discomfort overtook her whilst going round the dormitories in the execution of her duty. The dormitories were named after notable naval victories, it would not be difficult to decide on whose authority, and she was in Matapan when she was forced to clutch her swelling midriff and sit upon Macpherson's bed.

'I say, Mrs Williams, what's up?' asked Macpherson.

'I'm afraid I don't feel very well. Would you please find Mr Williams, and ask him to come up here?'

But it was Matron who collected her and bore her off to her room, sending for her anguished husband and ringing up the school doctor in the twinkling of an eye.

41

'I wonder what's wrong with her. She looked awfully pale,' said Macpherson.

'Miscarriage, of course,' announced Wilkinson. His father was a doctor, and he himself was the gynaecological expert in the Common Entrance form.

'Does that mean the baby'll pop out right now?' asked Smythe.

Assuming that Mr and Mrs Williams had gone into action extremely early in their married life, or even before that, Smythe had betted heavily on the baby's arrival before the end of October. This could be his big night.

'We don't pay up for a miscarriage, only a live birth,' announced Wilkinson pontifically.

He had gone very deeply into the matter, and had calculated that Christmas would be just about right. In deference to his superior knowledge, the swelling was already known as Noel, and was regarded by the C.E. form with an almost proprietary interest. A pay-out in October would have lowered his prestige considerably.

'Do you mean that all bets are off if it's a miscarriage?' asked Golightly in a tone of voice which seemed, superficially, to be rather too cheerful for such a sad occasion. He had been soured by the discovery that he had confused the gestation period of a human with that of a whale, and had picked on a date at least fourteen months ahead of anyone else. Here was an unexpected chance to recoup his losses, so naturally he saw the brighter side.

But further eavesdropping on the conversation in Matapan would be unprofitable, for Mrs Williams managed to hold her own, though with difficulty. What did transpire was that she was forced to give up her job at once, and Wintergreen was temporarily without an under–matron.

'I'll keep watch on my own until half-term,' said Matron to O.W., 'but you'd better find someone after that.'

'It won't be all that easy, Matron,' grumbled O.W. 'I'll begin to make tactful enquiries, though.'

'A little foresight would have avoided the problem altogether,' continued Matron, in a tone of voice which warned O.W. to make an engineering job of it.

He went into the staff room, on the off-chance that Tony might have one or two under-matrons available for him to select, and he found help in a slightly unexpected quarter.

'Well, sir,' Mike chipped in, 'if you are really stuck, I'm sure that my girlfriend would love to come.'

Everyone looked at him in some surprise, for they never thought of him as a possible source of supply.

'This sounds promising,' said O.W. 'Come along into my room and tell me all about her.'

On their way there, Mike wondered to himself whether O.W. would think much of his idea. It would be fun having Ann about the place, and he had already missed her company this term. They had known each other since they were in the same infants' class, and they thought that eventually they might marry, though there had been little talk of it as yet. Old Willerby's first question boomed out as soon as they reached his study.

'Well now, what's her name and what's she like?'

'Ann Pinkerton,' answered Mike, 'her father's a stockbroker, and she's very tough. She wants to be a policewoman.'

'How old is she?'

'Seventeen, sir, which means that she'll have to wait over a year before she can join the force.'

'And what about her education?'

'Grammar school, like me. She's three A levels, with a B in history.'

'That sounds very good. Would she fit in with us here?'

'I should say she'd fit in anywhere. I can't imagine many situations she couldn't deal with.'

'Is she good with small boys?'

'Well, she's a couple of small brothers – oh, and on occasion, I used to get her to help me scrub a first-former.'

'Scrub a first former?'

'Why, yes. It's a problem which we don't have at Wintergreen, but some grammar school boys have a shocking home background. He had to de-louse about three of them last year.'

'Really, Mike, you surprise me. And what's Miss Pinkerton doing now?'

'She's working in a factory, but she could walk out when she likes. I suppose she'd have to give a week's notice, but she could be here long before half-term.'

This sounded admirable to O.W., who did not relish the idea of Matron pacing the decks in solitary splendour, and giving him the benefit of a broadside from time to time. This prospective WPC, who took the de-lousing of small grammar school boys in her stride, would probably stand up well to the quarterdeck manner of her superior officer. Some under-matrons just weren't up to it, and O.W. could remember well the country parson's daughter who had fled back to the rectory within one week. O.W. had been forced to listen to one sermon from Matron on the subject of decadence in modern youth, and to another from the girl's father on the milk of human kindness. He was not going to employ any delicate flowers if he could help it.

Just then, an idea struck him, and he delicately questioned Mike.

'Now what's your position with her? The term "girlfriend" can cover quite a lot these days, you know.'

Mike was a little taken aback, but recovered quickly.

'Well, sir, I don't sleep with her, if that's what you mean. We've been Youth Hostelling together, but the sexes are kept apart there during the most likely mating times.'

O.W. looked suitably relieved.

'I am very glad to hear it. We can't have that sort of thing at Wintergreen. Morals are getting far too slack these days. Right then, I'll offer her the job. What's her address?'

'I'll give it you, but would you like me to ring her up now, and warn her what it's all about?'

'Yes, Mike. That's a good idea, and if she approves I'll write off at once.'

Without demur, Ann said that she would be delighted to come. She could probably start within ten days if she sent in her notice at the factory on the Monday, which caused O.W. to rejoice. He felt that in ten days Matron would hardly have time to work up tremendous pressure in her boilers, and this would be far more restful for him. Four days later, he took pride in announcing to Matron that her new assistant would be arriving on Monday, 21st October. He was more than gratified by her reply.

'How splendid,' she said. 'She'll be starting on Trafalgar Day, so the tide will be just right for her.'

'She'll be in time to splice the mainbrace with you. Now don't fill her up with too much rum.'

'A little tot never did anyone any harm,' answered Matron, who always saw to it that the staff drank a toast to the Admiral's memory. Even O.W., who didn't care for rum, was made to drink it. He reacted to it as the boys reacted to her nasty medicines – and with equally little success.

The latest addition to the Wintergreen staff started her journey north at seven o'clock in the morning on Trafalgar Day. She was a tall, well-built girl, with fair hair, a firm chin and very little make–up. She had sent on her heavy luggage, and was hitchhiking. This was not because she was short of cash, but because she liked it. Her parents did not like the idea, particularly after she had told them that on one occasion she had had to sling a truck driver out of his own cab when he got too fresh. She was an expert at judo, and she was in the habit of wearing heavy climbing boots when on the road, which this particular driver considered darned unfair.

Ann was able to reach the Great North Road by furniture van, whereupon she transferred to a high–powered car, whose driver was in a hurry. This took her to within ten miles of Elmet long before lunch, and her luck continued to hold. She was dropped in a lay-by, in which was resting a very striking vehicle. It was an aged Rolls-Royce van, painted purple and black. She stopped to admire it, noticing that on its side was a strange device. An enormous tortoise, on which a particularly mad-looking hare was apparently dancing, took up a good square yard of the gleaming coachwork. The hare was holding a bottle of medicine in one pad and a large apron in the other, whilst the whole was capped by the three letters M.A.D. On the door of the van was printed discreetly: 'M.A. Dalton & Nephew, Wholesale Chemists, Morcargate, Elmet'.

Ann walked once round this conveyance, and was start-ing a second circle, when an ancient gentleman appeared from behind a hedge, adjusting his clothing a little ostentatiously.

'Morning, luv,' said the apparition, 'a proper treat, aren't she?'

The foreign accent, for Ann had never been in Yorkshire, was difficult, but she managed to cope with it all right.

'I think she's lovely. Could you give me a lift in her to Elmet?'

'Ay, I could, but I shan't get back while five. I've another seventeen drops yet.'

'Oh, what a shame. That's a bit late for me, because I've got to find my way to Wintergreen.'

'Did you say Wintergreen, luv?'

'Yes, it's a village about ten miles from Elmet.'

'Ay, I know it is. I'm going there myself. It'll take nigh on two hours though.'

'Splendid. Will you take me, please?'

'Ay. You're welcome.'

It was the work of a moment for Ann to heave her bag into the back amongst the packages, and to establish herself in the very comfortable passenger's seat. Dalton's van moved silently out of the lay-by.

'Isn't she a beauty? Why, I can hardly hear the engine,' said Ann.

The ancient mariner positively purred. Here was a young lady who really appreciated his charge.

'Ay,' he said. 'She was built to last, she was. Belonged to a lord afore Dalton's bought her – and that was over thirty years ago. There's nowt like an old Rolls.'

'And how long have you been driving her?'

'Why, all thirty years, to be sure. I go back to 'orse vans, I do, but we 'ad to move wi'times.'

'Well, you've looked after her well.'

'Ay, that I have, luv. She's as near perfect as can be. Ne'er a breakdown in all those years – just a puncture now and again to show she's 'uman.'

'No accidents either?'

'Well, went through t'edge once. Met a 'erd of cows on a blind corner, and took avoiding action.'

'That's not too bad in thirty years.'

'There was another time, luv. During the war, a Yank ran into me in one o' they jeeps. Scratched t'spoon out of t'are's 'and, he did – but t'jeep was a total loss, he was.'

The driver's name was Charlie Wise, and for purposes of clarity the total loss of 'h's and complete syllables is not recorded. Sometimes, the sentences had to be repeated more than once before Ann could get their meaning. She learnt a lot about the delivery of goods that day, and she helped poor Charlie, whose lumbago was giving him trouble.

What he called a 'six 'oler', six very large bottles in a wooden container, was taken up a long garden path to a doctor's surgery, and it needed both of them to cope with that. Village stores received patent medicines and disposable nappies, toilet requisites and hot water bottles. There was one gigantic carton which would only just go through the narrow doorway of a shop whose main stock in trade appeared to be Liquorice Allsorts.

'All t'ladies need 'em,' said Charlie laconically, as he helped Ann in with it.

At one point, they made a three-mile detour to deliver one small package, and Ann immediately knew what was in it. It was a neat, plain carton, which quite disgusted Charlie.

'Fancy, all this ruddy way for a packet of...'

'I know,' interrupted Ann, 'I've just spent six weeks packing the things.'

'Have you, by God,' said Charlie, 'and what might you be doing at Wintergreen?'

'I've got a job as under-matron at the school.'

'Rather you than me,' said Charlie, 'yon Miss Blake's a proper terror.'

'I've heard all about her from my boyfriend. He seems to get on all right with her.'

'Good luck to you, anyway – and I think you may need it.'

Slowly the goods disappeared, but empties helped to fill up the space. Just before they reached Wintergreen, Ann jumped into the back, and changed into something a little more suitable than her climbing attire for a state entry into her new place of work. Then they drove through the gatehouse of Wintergreen School, swung round the famous lawn and stopped in front of the imposing main entrance. Ann felt that she had seldom seen a more lovely setting; she was sure that she was going to enjoy Wintergreen a good deal more than the rubber factory.

4

'Now then, Mr Wise,' said a deep female voice from the steps, 'what do you think you're doing?'

'Afternoon, Miss Blake,' said Charlie.

'Side door for tradesmen – you know that quite well.'

'Ay, I'll go there wit'goods, but I've got a young lady for you.'

'Good afternoon,' said Ann, climbing out. 'Mr Wise gave me a lift. I'm Ann Pinkerton.'

'Oh, you are, are you? Let's have a good look at you.'

What Matron saw evidently pleased her. So many under-matrons needed the paint washing off their faces and dye out of their hair before they were presentable. She shook her warmly by the hand, being gratified to discover that Ann did not wince at her iron grip. Indeed, Matron encountered a very healthy resistance to it.

'Your luggage came this morning. What have you got there?'

She eyed the boots critically, for they were loose.

'Oh, just a bag and my boots. I always wear them when I am hitchhiking – but I do climb a little too.'

'Well, put them on the deck there. Let's see what Dalton's have sent us.'

They walked to the side door, where Charlie was dutifully waiting.

'Four 'oler for you, Miss Blake, and a carton of odds and sods too,' he said.

'Really,' said Matron, 'that's not how I should describe it. And what's in the four-holer?'

49

'Two wins of Dalton's number twenty-five, and one each of number two and number three.'

'What on earth's a win?' asked Ann curiously.

'Short for Winchester – a term used in the trade,' said Matron, heaving out an enormous bottle and examining it.

'I thought a Winchester was a repeating rifle,' said Ann.

'Have a swig of that lot of number three, and you won't repeat it,' chipped in Charlie. 'It's 'orrible.'

'Best aperient on the market,' said Matron. 'Not even the most obstinate bowels can resist it.'

'What's the significance of the numbers?'

'Three opens, two closes and twenty-five stops coughs – suddenly and completely,' said Matron.

'Twenty-five's 'orrible too,' went on Charlie. 'Now twenty–eight's real nice – I take that myself.'

'With a stiff whisky, I've no doubt. It's not so good with boys, though; I've tried it. They like it so much that they'd go on coughing until the Swiss Navy owns a couple of battleships. Now number twenty-five stops them in their tracks.'

'How many numbers are there, Charlie?' asked Ann.

'We go up to thirty-seven, but they're dying out. More's the pity, I say – it'll all be penicillin and suchlike soon.'

With that, he collected up some empties and prepared to leave. Ann wondered to herself just what sort of a place Dalton's could be, where thirty-seven mixtures were brewed and where so many different things were sold. She was even more puzzled by Matron's next question, called out at Charlie's hindquarters, as he was shutting the doors of the van.

'When are you bringing the hounds?' she asked. 'It must be soon after half-term.'

'Let's see, Miss Blake. It must be the second Saturday in November. The Colonel's sending the cards out this week, anyway.'

Matron explained that Mr Wise was a man of parts. When not working as a van driver, he was kennelman and huntsman to Colonel Dalton's basset hounds. They put in an annual appearance at Wintergreen, much to the delight of the boys and the amusement of the local hare population.

'We're having a grand season,' went on Charlie, 'we've nearly killed once, and they've left t'sheep alone so far. Well, it's time I made a move. Thank you, luv, for all your help.'

'And thank you for the lift,' said Ann. 'I've never been in a Rolls before; it was fabulous.'

Charlie moved off, and the two ladies picked up the goods. It was significant that Ann took the 'wins', whilst her superior officer was content with the lighter package. They put the goods in the surgery, and then Ann was taken to see Old Willerby. Between then and tea, she unpacked, being assisted by Matron, who wanted to have a look at her attire just to make quite sure that she would be clad in the correct rig of the day. A clean white overall was handed out, and Matron announced her satisfaction when Ann was safely buttoned up inside it. At tea, an informal meal to which the staff drifted when they felt inclined, Ann met all of them. Matron left her for half an hour, which gave her the opportunity to tell Mike about her journey, especially the last stages of it.

'I hope you'll feel strong enough for the party this evening after all that,' he said. 'You're a historian, so you ought to know what day we are to celebrate as Matron herself.'

'Let me see, Mike. Matron ... yes, it must be something naval. Could it be Trafalgar Day?'

'It could be, and it is. When the boys are safely in their hammocks, we go to Matron's room. No excuses, and neat rum's the only drink.'

'That seems quite a good idea. But tell me, is Miss Fellowes up to it?'

'What, Flip Flap? I really don't know. She's probably more incoherent than usual after a sniff at the bottle. Let's ask her.'

He caught her eye and called out:

'Hey, Florence, what do you think of rum as a drink?'

She came over, and all the cares of the world flowed from her.

'It's too bad,' she burbled, 'it really is. Rum's so strong, and Matron won't let us have any water, or anything. It honestly makes me quite dizzy just to sip it – and she gives us so much. Those tumblers of hers hold such a lot. Now, Ann, I may call you Ann, mayn't I? You must be careful; you probably aren't used to anything so intoxicating. If you like, I'll tell her you are teetotal – but I don't know that that will do much good, since Matron is so strong-willed. We had a master once who thought that strong drink was a sin. Two of the others held him down, and Matron poured. That was many years ago, but I shall never forget the poor man's face. He was a conscientious objector too, and Matron was very rude to him about that. Though I don't see why one shouldn't be entitled to one's own opinions. I've often thought that if we all objected enough there would be no wars. Oh dear, I shall be so glad when it's all over. I have a whole pile of corrections to do, essays, you know, and they take such a terrible time.'

She waffled on for some minutes, and then drifted away to pour out her woes into other ears. Tony, who had been listening, joined Ann and Mike.

'Don't you believe her,' he said, 'she swigs it down, and has a wonderful time, though two years out of three Matron has to put her to bed before the party's over. She always sets an essay for Trafalgar Day – you'd think she'd learn, but the silly old thing doesn't. The rest of us set work which is easy to correct.'

'This is going to be quite an experience,' said Ann, 'but,

first of all, I've got to get down to work. I've met the staff – and now for the little horrors.'

As she said this, in came Matron to collect her, for it was nearly time for the boys' tea.

'Out pipes, hands carry on with your work,' she roared. 'Come along, Ann. I'll show you the ropes tonight, and you can take tea tomorrow.'

She whisked her away at the rate of knots, leaving the men to talk.

'Will she be able to stand the pace?' asked Ken, who had been listening. 'She seems quite a lass, but she's gone in at the deep end all right.'

'Oh, she'll be OK,' answered Mike. 'She's as tough as old boots. I shall never forget when she took me round the Snowdon Horseshoe, for it darned nearly killed me. I suppose you know it like the back of your hand, Ken. I wouldn't call it a half-day excursion, would you?'

'Snowdon Horseshoe?' said Ken. 'It's not too bad – I took Macpherson and Duffield round last half-term. We scrambled up Tryfan the next day to wear off the stiffness.'

Macpherson was tough, but Duffield seemed hardly the type. He was the brains of the school, rather small and weedy, and with large round glasses.

'Duffield – how did he do? I shouldn't have thought that climbing was his cup of tea.'

'You'd be surprised,' answered Ken. 'He slowed us up a little, I must admit, but his theoretical knowledge was astounding. He never stopped telling us what we had to do, and he has since adopted the attitude that without him we should have been utterly lost.'

'Didn't you say that he would be going with you to the Lake District at Easter?' asked Tony.

'That depends. Not unless I can get someone to go with me. Are you coming again?'

'Unfortunately not. I enjoyed last year, but there is a course

I must go on, and I ought to spend the rest of the time with my mother. She doesn't get any younger, you know.'

'Well then, Mike. What about you?'

'Yes, I'm interested, but there could be complications. Where do we stay, and how big will the party be?'

'Youth Hostels, so it's right up your street. We wouldn't have more than ten boys, probably more like half a dozen.'

'When do you want to know for sure?'

'Well, I'd have to do the booking soon after half-term. The boys will see their parents then, and I'll write off after that.'

'Good Lord,' said Mike, 'that seems a long way ahead.'

'Oh, I don't know about that,' said Tony. There's a hell of a scrum with school parties at Easter, and you have to book months ahead.'

'I never realised that, though I've been hostelling in the Easter holidays. We generally stick to the smaller hostels. Do you know Black Sail?'

'Yes, that's my sort,' said Ken, 'but the big ones, like Keswick and Ambleside, positively seethe with school parties.'

'Yes,' went on Tony, 'I was amazed at the hordes there. They varied in both their manners and their methods of passing the time.'

'A lot of the boys and girls seemed to be mooching around wearing slippers, never went off a main road and were obviously looking forward to the return home,' remarked Ken.

'That may be true,' said Mike, 'but there are a lot of good school parties – even mixed ones.'

'Agreed, but a poor school party is enough to put anyone off. What did you think of our lot, Tony?'

'Seemed to be able to do a man's day, provided that they travelled light. I don't think that Wainwright could ever have met us; he's a bit rude about school parties.'

'You mean the great Mr Wainwright?' asked Mike.

'None other. He's a real public benefactor, and his books will be a joy to millions.'

'I know. I've just bought the Western Fells.'

'Oh, I've got all seven. They're superb,' said Ken.

By this time, the boys' tea was over, and the bell for prep cut short their conversation.

'Oh, damn, I'm on duty,' called out Ken on his way to the door. 'Just you think it over, and let me know in a week or so. I'll have to get cracking by then.'

'Up spirits!' boomed Matron, and then she charged the glasses.

'Now then, belay that racket everyone,' she called out, her duty done. 'No defaulters, I see, and you've all got your tots.'

She stood near the fireplace, clutching a winchester to her ample bosom. It, the winchester, not the bosom, was labelled 'Nelson's Blood', but more than one guest hoped that there was no residue of Dalton's number three adhering to the sides. Everyone, even Mrs Willerby, was present, and there were two visitors. The first was Jack Wright, complete with 'croicks Makalache' and other medals. He always came along by virtue of his wartime association with Matron. The other was an aged parson, the local vicar. He came up to the school twice a week to teach divinity, which made his presence on this solemn occasion obligatory, but he also was a wartime acquaintance of Matron's. He was called 'Father' by all of them, which pinpoints his churchmanship, and introduced to Ann by Matron as 'my old friend Father Mirfield'. He was a stout little man, with white hair and a very lively twinkle in his old eyes.

Matron gave the toast to the memory of Horatio, Lord Nelson, Vice Admiral of the White, in a voice of thunder, a voice which carried through the dividing wall into Matapan, where seven tooth mugs, filled to the brim with dandelion and burdock, were clutched in seven small hands, The mugs were clinked together, not without a little of the precious liquid being spilt in the process, and then the contents were downed in one. The anguished look of anxiety on Golightly's face was matched in Matron's room by that of Old Willerby, but Matron was watching him like a hawk. This enabled Mrs Willerby to take advantage of Matron's momentary distraction, and neatly tip the majority of the contents of her tumbler into a plant pot at her elbow containing a well–loved cyclamen. The rest of them drank deeply, and Matron was round again with the bottle before they could recover.

'Oh, no thank you. I couldn't, I really couldn't. It's so strong, Matron,' protested Flip Flap, but it was noticeable that she held out her glass for more – and got it.

'There you are, the old fraud,' said Tony to Mike. 'Didn't I tell you what would happen?'

'The lady protests too much, methinks,' answered Mike.

'*Hamlet*, act three, scene two,' broke in Topsy. He had his attaché case with him, and was in excellent form.

The party continued fast and furious, and nobody noticed a knocking at the door, faint at first but more persistent and urgent as the moments passed.

'What's that, what's that? I'm sure I heard somebody knocking. What can have happened?' said Flip Flap at last, quite clearly of the opinion that at the very least the school was on fire.

There was a silence, interrupted by an almighty bang on the panelling.

'Probably a woodpecker; take no notice,' said Jack Wright reassuringly.

At this point, the door was opened cautiously, and a small figure in pyjamas appeared. In spite of his size and his clothing, Duffield had the air of an ambassadorial butler.

'Duty monitor reporting,' he said in an important voice. 'I am sorry to say, Matron, that Golightly has been sick.'

'Oh, he has, has he? Well, you'd better start swabbing the decks, I'm not on watch, but I'll come along in a minute.'

To say that Duffield was scandalised would be putting it mildly. It was his duty, he knew, to pass on the glad news, but the situation, grave as it was, did not call for further action on his part.

'Me, Matron? But...'

'An engineering job, Duffield. I'll have no mutiny here,' started Matron, but the situation was saved by Ann, who felt that perhaps her superior officer was being unduly harsh.

'I'll come,' she said, and made towards the door.

'Clean sheets in the airing cupboard,' called out Matron, thinking that her new assistant was at least worthy of leading rank.

'Bring me a mop and bucket, Duffield,' Ann said kindly as she went out with him, 'and then go back to bed.'

'Thank you, Miss Pinkerton,' he answered, his dignity restored. 'I dispatched Macpherson for the materials, and they are already in Matapan.'

With that, he continued on his way, feeling that after all he had done his duty as befitted the deputy head boy.

When Ann arrived in Matapan, mopping up operations were already under way. Macpherson was pushing the mop around in a desultory kind of way, and Wilkinson was attending to the invalid, a basin at the ready.

'It's quite all right, Miss Pinkerton,' said Macpherson. 'He missed the bedclothes beautifully.'

'That's a good thing,' said Ann. 'Give me that mop, and hop into bed.'

It was not long before she had cleared up the mess, and Macpherson was loud in her praises.

'Why, you're nearly as good as Matron; that's an engineering job all right. Mrs Williams would probably have been sick too.'

'That's enough from you, and now, Golightly, how do you feel?'

'Fine, thank you. You know it tasted just as good coming up as it did going down.'

'Don't be so disgusting, Golightly. By the way, what was it that went down, and came up?'

'Oh, the grog, Miss Pinkerton. Please don't tell Old ... I mean Mr Willerby.'

'I don't see why I shouldn't. Would he be very cross if I did?'

'You bet he would,' said Wilkinson. 'He'd beat the lot of us – in our pyjamas too – and we're only drinking to Nelson's memory like the staff.'

'But the staff aren't going to be sick. At least, I hope they aren't. I'm not clearing up after them, anyway.'

'But you won't tell Mr Willerby, please?' begged Golightly. 'You see it was my fault, and they'd all have sore bottoms.'

'Very well, not this time, but you get to sleep now.'

With that, Ann turned off the light, and, having removed all traces of the debauchery, she returned to the party.

'All well?' asked Mike. 'You've just come back in time. Jack's going to sing to us.'

It wasn't often that Jack got away from his duties at the Green Dragon, and he was making an evening of it. Unfortunately, his repertoire of songs consisted entirely of the type which is not usually heard either in mixed company or within hearing of preparatory school dormitories.

'How about "Roll me Over in the Clover"?' he asked after four or five other suggestions had been vetoed.

Matron hummed the tune over to herself meditatively.

'No, it won't do,' she said at last. 'Miss Fellowes would not approve.'

It was quite certain that by this time Miss Fellowes did not give a damn, in fact the time was approaching when she would have to be escorted bedwards, but Jack bowed to the command of his superior officer.

'Very well then. I'll give you "La Faridondaine". It's in French, so the words don't matter.'

Matron, who couldn't be bothered with foreign lingos, gave her consent, and Jack was soon singing in excruciating French. He probably never knew what the song meant himself, having learnt it off parrot-fashion from some French matelots over twenty years before. All joined in the rousing chorus, which started '*Frotte ton cul contre le mien*', the vicar's accent being especially pleasing to Tony's trained ear. This was hardly surprising, since Father Mirfield had been in French-speaking territory for some forty years of his long ministry.

'I don't know what all that was about,' said O.W. to him afterwards. 'Something classical would be more in my line.'

'Well, it wasn't edifying, but I'd call it fairly harmless, especially when Jack's singing.'

'I'm quite certain that we'd never have got that miserable North Ender to join in if I'd appointed him to the living.'

Old Willerby was referring to an eminent evangelical, to whom he had been on the point of offering the living some two years before. To those not up in the liturgy of the Church of England, the more extreme evangelicals take the communion service from the north end of the altar, or Holy Table as they insist on calling it. This matters a very great deal to them, and there is no reason whatsoever why they should not be allowed to do it.

'I never could understand why you first considered a Protestant, and then offered the living to an Anglo–Catholic like me,' said Father Mirfield.

'Well, the last fellow was a washout – no congregation,

no life in the parish. He was a middle of the road parson, dull as ditch water, who cut no ice at all. I wanted an extremist, either a "prot" or a "spike" would do, to stir up. The sword of the Lord and of Gideon, you know.'

'So you picked on Father Brining?'

'Father? He wouldn't like that much. Yes, I picked on him. Although he was filling his London church, he was badly in need of a rest after years of overwork.'

'But surely, he'd have filled this church too.'

'Oh yes, I think he would, but the fellow was quite impossible.'

'Surely not?'

'Yes, Father, quite impossible, he's a damned prig. We had him up one Sunday, and he preached at us for twenty-seven minutes – good stuff, perhaps, but far too long – and then I had him for the night.'

'He wasn't a perfect guest, I take it.'

'He wouldn't smoke, he wouldn't drink, he wouldn't gamble, he wouldn't enjoy himself on the Sabbath, or any other day as far as I could judge,' said O.W. bitterly.

'That must have made him rather a wet blanket.'

'Yes, but I was prepared to put up with that. A man's entitled to his opinions, I suppose. What settled his hash was that he expected me to do the same, me, the patron of the living. What damned cheek!' and O.W. puffed away at his pipe, taking sips at his rum, which by this time was beginning to taste rather better to him.

'So you swapped him for a spike, and got yourself in a worse mess.'

'Nonsense, Father. It's you who have filled the church again, and I think your God's the same as mine – though at times I did have my doubts. Personally, I'm all for moderation in all things ecclesiastical. I'm good old traditional C of E, but I must admit that it didn't work here, and your brand of high jinks does.'

'You know, Squire, I don't think I'll ever make a good Catholic of you – or Matron, for that matter – but we're bound to have our failures.'

'I have my doubts too, Father, but your efforts are appreciated, you know.'

'Oh, thank you – and the day may yet come when I persuade you to act as thurifer.'

'What, Father, the chap who swings the incense around? You'd better ask Matron if you're short of one. She'd make an engineering job of it.'

'She isn't eligible, and you are.'

'If you tell Matron that, Father, she'd probably insist – and you'd make a notable conversion.'

'What's that?' called out Matron. 'Are you two taking my name in vain?'

'No,' said O.W. 'We're just putting it forward for incense swinging on Sunday.'

'Certainly not. You'll never get me flirting with Rome like that. The very idea!'

When Matron did go to the village church, which wasn't all that often, as she always conjured up a pile of darning when pressed, she remained a pillar of Protestantism, stiff as a ramrod when others genuflected, hands held steady when others made the sign of the cross. To do otherwise was flirting with Rome, and by no manner of means an engineering proposition. Old Willerby, on the other hand, felt that when in Rome he should set a good example to the boys and do as the Romans do.

'Never mind, my dear,' said Father Mirfield. 'I respect your views, wrong as they are.'

Just after this, he looked at his watch, and noticed with a start that it was long past the time when he normally retired to bed.

'Good gracious me,' he called out. 'It's time I left, or I'll never be up for mass in the morning.'

Matron stiffened at the word, but managed to refrain from comment with an effort.

'But before I go,' he continued, 'I have a toast for you.'

The company was all attention, and several of the more seasoned topers made quite sure that there was something in their glasses.

'Most of you know,' went on Father Mirfield when all were ready, 'that there was another naval victory in an October of more recent date. I refer, of course, to the capture of Maquemique by HMS *Beetle* in World War Two, and I ask you to drink to *Beetle* and her gallant commanding officer.'

Father Mirfield had a reputation for tact, which accounted, in some measure for the size of his congregations. Both Matron and Jack Wright, though they might not be very regular members of his flock, would certainly be in church next Sunday.

On the vicar's departure, the gathering broke up, and Mike and Ann decided that a little fresh air was needed. It was a fine night, with a full moon shining benevolently upon them. This, combined with the effects of the rum, caused them to walk hand in hand through the gateway, a fact which was noticed by Matron, who was gazing out of her window. The moon and the rum must have affected her too, for there was a look on her leathery face which every member of the Common entrance form would quite definitely have called soppy.

But apart from the hand-holding, romance and young love were not particularly noticeable. It was mainly about the school that they talked. Mike was already very much of the team, although he had been barely a month at Wintergreen. In a small prep school one soon develops a sense of almost feudal loyalty, something which is far more difficult to achieve at a large state school. Without it, the term would have seemed unbearably long. O.W. made a point of seeing that each member of his staff had one afternoon per week away from the place, but there was plenty to do each weekend. The 'Thank God for Friday' attitude, which is manifest in so many state schools, simply did not exist.

'Well, Ann, what do you think of us?' asked Mike.

'Oh, Mike, it's grand. I'm quite sure I'm going to be very happy here. I've fallen in love with the place already.'

'So have I,' said Mike. 'I could live my whole life very happily in an atmosphere like this.'

'Would you stay on if you had the chance, or come back after you've been to university?'

'No, at least not until I've seen the world from other angles. There's a certain lack of reality about the place.'

'It's certainly very different from my factory.'

'What was it like there really? You seemed to enjoy it from your letters.'

'It was an experience, and well worth it. A long spell would have driven me stark staring bonkers, and six weeks of packing rubber goods was quite long enough. You know, there just can't be any more dirty stories on the subject which I haven't heard at least twice.'

'But what are the people like? I don't really know very much about working-class parents – though we've both mixed with their more intelligent children.'

'They're the salt of the earth, but so stupid sometimes that I could knock their silly heads together.'

They spoke of their activities since they had last met, and Mike told Ann of the school party to the Lake District in the spring. He said that he had been asked by Ken to go with him, but that he had not committed himself.

'I told him that there were complications,' he said, 'but I didn't say that I had already fixed to go hostelling with you.'

'But, Mike, you must go. I don't mind a bit if our trip falls through.'

'But I do, Ann. What would you say to coming too?'

'I'm all for it, but do under-matrons go climbing with the boys in the holidays?'

'Well, if they don't I don't either,' said Mike. 'I'll have a word with Ken in the morning, and see what he says.'

'Any ideas about half-term?' asked Ann.

In a small boarding school, the half-term break, about which Ann had already heard a good deal, is something to which both staff and boys look forward with even greater pleasure than their counterparts at a day school.

'Oh, I did think about going home, but now you're here we might do something together. You won't want to be off south again so soon, will you?'

'No, but oughtn't you to go? There's a large Youth Hostel in York, and I want to see the town.'

'It's a bit of a fag going home for such a short time, only Friday morning until Monday night. Let's see the sights of York together.'

'OK, Mike. As it's a weekend, I suppose we'd better book,' said Ann.

Well pleased with this arrangement, they returned to the school, where both of them slept the sleep of the just.

5

'OK,' said Ken, after Mike had explained the situation to him. 'We'll sign Ann on too for the Lake District. I've had a scout round already, and there aren't many seniors who want to come. What do you think about Anderson and Stevenson? They'll both be eleven by then, and they're dead keen.'

'I don't know a fat lot about the capabilities of small boys, I'm afraid. They're a bit young, aren't they?'

'Could be. I tell you what, I'll give them a test on the moors, and see how they go. Hugh can darned well spare Stevenson for one afternoon.'

'All the same, he'll whine like blazes, won't he?'

'I don't see why he should,' answered Ken.

'You mark my words, you'll be slowing Stevenson down, or some such nonsense. These dedicated games players have no sense of proportion. I had my bellyful with rude remarks over my cross-country running from the football pundits when I was at school.'

'Well, my afternoon off is Friday, and there's no match on Saturday. I'll fix it all up with O.W., and that will spike Hugh's guns.'

'That's a bit dirty, isn't it?' queried Mike.

'Just gamesmanship. He'd do the same to me and think nothing of it.'

'How far were you thinking of taking them?'

'Oh, ten to twelve miles should be enough, I think, and we'll put them over the climb too.'

'What climb?'

'It's a course which I thought up for the Scouts. Over the junior changing-room, down through the boot-hole, up again onto the lab roof and down the drainpipe by the kitchen window. I use a rope just to impress O.W. and show how careful I am, but there's no need really.'

'You'd better put Ann and me through it too; we may not be up to scratch.'

'Don't you worry. The whole party's going over before final acceptance.'

Mike could not picture a climbing venture on these lines at his old school. Whatever mischief staff and boys got up to, an organised climbing expedition over the rooftops would not be tolerated either by the headmaster or the Local Education Authority. Nobody thought twice about it at Wintergreen; that was the beauty of a small boarding school, whose day did not finish abruptly for most people with the bell for the end of afternoon work.

When they hear about Anderson and Stevenson's trip, the rest of the third form volunteered in a body for the ordeal. Here was an opportunity for avoiding work which was not to be missed, and a remarkable enthusiasm for walking was suddenly displayed. Anderson and Stevenson, however, were quite definitely the only starters. There was very strong opposition from Hugh, as Mike had foretold, and one would have thought from his attitude that the walk had been contrived by Ken for the sole purpose of robbing the first fifteen of a brilliant scrum half.

'This sort of thing does untold harm,' said Hugh. 'Anyway, I'm having a practice on Friday, and I must have Stevenson.'

'That's rot,' said Ken. 'A good long walk over the heather will improve his stamina no end. You have the boy down on the field every blinking afternoon, and a rest from it will do him the world of good.'

'Ken, you're the limit. The whole thing is most inconvenient.'

'I'm sorry, chum, but I'm giving up ten days of my holidays to take the boys on the trip, and it's essential that I should know whether Stevenson can walk or not. So far, all that he's done this term has been to run a yard or two and then bury his face in the mud. If you can think of a better time for the trip, I'll see what I can do about making use of it – but it'll have to be before half-term.'

They went over every second of the ten days between the present moment and the dawn of Friday week, and Ken's original timing was the only possible one. A very grudging approval was eventually given by Hugh, so O.W. did not have to be brought in as an arbitrator.

Immediately after morning school on the Friday, the three travellers collected sandwiches and bundled themselves into Ken's car, a motor caravan of venerable appearance. All three had rucksacks, Ken's containing the necessities of the expedition. In theirs the two boys carried a spare sweater and a brick. Ken felt that the ballast could be thrown out if things were going badly, but that the fact that they were carrying a bit of weight would give them some idea of what their Easter holiday would entail. Both Mike and Ann watched them drive off, and Ann at once remarked in a rather scandalised voice:

'Did you see what they had on their feet?'

'Why, gym shoes. I believe that Ken orders them shoes with bars on the bottom, fell shoes I think he called them, for the trip.'

'But they ought to be in boots. I can't understand it.'

'You'd better ask Ken when he comes back. I know you can't be separated from those seven league things of yours, but I'm not wedded to mine.'

It was long after dark when they got back, and the two boys were tired though in excellent spirits. They were sent up straight to their dormitory, Jutland by name.

'Well, how did you enjoy the voyage?' Matron asked them.

'It was smashing, Matron,' said Stevenson.

Perhaps owing to his training on the rugger field, he was carrying his brick around with him like a ball.

'What do you want with that thing in the dormitory?' asked Matron, pointing accusingly at the brick.

'Please, Matron, this is the brick I had in my rucksack. You feel it – isn't it heavy?'

Matron felt it obligingly.

'Well, you can't turn in with it, my lad. No bricks in Jutland, or I'll have you keelhauled.'

With that, she opened the window, and slung it out into the night.

'Oh, Matron. What have you done?' moaned the owner of the brick. He got up the next morning rather earlier than usual, and was happily able to retrieve the brick from a flower bed. He put it in his desk, and a few surreptitious looks at it during both the Latin and the English lessons helped him to pass the morning agreeably.

Anderson, on the other hand, did not attempt to set up his brick as a graven image. His mind dwelt on the fabulous hot dogs which had been a reward for their endeavours.

'Please, Matron,' he told her, 'Mr Padgett's a wizard cook. We had hot dogs, and the sausages were much better than the muck we have on Wednesdays.'

'That's enough, Anderson. These were school bangers you had anyway.'

'Well, Matron, Mr Padgett made a better engineering job than Cook does.'

'Oh, he did, did he? It's probably because you were so hungry. Have your bath now, or you'll be adrift.'

The same evening, Ann got on to Ken about the lack of boots.

'Surely you don't wear gym shoes for walking,' she said.

'Why, yes. I'm used to them. Actually, they are fell shoes, with bars on the soles and heels.'

'You must be a freak, and do you make the boys wear them too?'

'Oh, no. I don't make them, but I advise it strongly.'

'Aren't you frightened of accidents, sprained ankles and soon?'

'No. Mind you, I'm always prepared for the worst, with yards and yards of crêpe bandage just in case. And I'm prepared to carry a casualty.'

'And how often does that happen?'

'Never so far, touch wood.'

'It all seems very odd to me,' said Ann, quite unconvinced.

'It did to Matron too when I first took a party about five years ago. There were eight boys on the trip, and six of them were wearing the most imposing new boots. The other two wore fell shoes, and I barely escaped a court martial for letting them.'

'And has she changed her mind?'

'Yes. She had to,' went on Ken. 'The six wearers of boots collected the most frightful blisters the first day, and carried the boots round their necks for the rest of the trip. The fell shoe wearers were quite all right, and I've never had trouble with them from that day to this.'

'But they were new boots. It would never have happened if they had run them in.'

'I quite agree, but blisters are not the only trouble. A small boy who suddenly puts on socking great boots alters his centre of gravity, exhausts himself with the extra weight and trips over himself as well as obstacles in this path.'

'But this is heresy. Why do all the experts say that boots are so essential?'

'I suspect because it is a very long time since they were nippers themselves.'

'That can't be right.'

'The experts are divided, you know, over this point of footwear. On the way to Everest in 1953, many of the party wore gym shoes on the march – and you couldn't say that they lacked experience.'

Ann looked so shattered that Ken added:

'Anyway, a boy used to boots is all right. I wouldn't discourage the wearer of a pair which are really well run in. It is, however, an expensive item for the parents of a growing lad. Yours may last for years, but Golightly and company are growing out of theirs all the time.'

'Yes, I see your point there,' said Ann grudgingly.

'There is one other aspect. Can you imagine Golightly looking after this boots properly? You spend time and loving care on their preservation, but he would be losing his half the time, and borrowing someone else's.'

'From the little that I have seen of Golightly,' admitted Ann, 'I should say that you are not far wrong. I may even be converted by the time the expedition is over.'

The great climb was fixed for Sunday afternoon, but first of all, the events of the morning service are worthy of recording. Wintergreen had its own chapel, what the guidebook called a mediaeval gem of the perpendicular period. Actually, there were considerably older features not entirely obliterated by later work. Each weekday, morning and evening, the school met there for prayers, and an occasional communion service was held there. On Sundays, however, the school went to worship at the parish church.

Under Mirfield's predecessor, this had been a weekly penance for everyone, but now the majority of the school looked forward to it. Even those whose family background caused them to have few religious beliefs, and it was to be regretted that the number was increasing, could hardly claim that there was ever a dull moment.

Not far short of a quarter of the school took a very active

part in the proceedings. Of the fifteen or so trebles and altos in the choir, a good dozen were always members of the school. They mixed well with the village lads who made up numbers, and O.W. would have been most upset if they hadn't. A ruff, with a cassock beneath a spotless cotta (known as a short surplice so as not to offend Protestant ears) acted as levellers. It is improbable that the little gentlemen of the school could be distinguished from the little proletarians from the village. Coached by Flip Flap, who was organist and lady choirmaster, they made a cheerful noise.

To add to this, there were servers and acolytes of every shape and size. The boys were well trained, and they loved it. Whether their activities were considered just the ticket or else pantomime in poor taste, nobody could deny that the boys took a far greater interest in this 'Catholic' form of worship. A good Protestant has every right to disapprove strongly, but he can produce nothing to touch it for excitement and sheer activity. It is extremely good for small boys to sit still and behave themselves, but they are far happier moving around. If they do have to sit still, they appreciate plenty to look at – and under Father Mirfield the sanctuary was a positive hive of activity.

At the Green Dragon, the school was halted by O.W. He did not approve of his flock walking in crocodile, but he liked them both to go and to return from church in a more or less organised body.

'Stop, boys,' he roared.

'Stop,' shouted well over seventy shrill voices. It was inconceivable that anyone had not heard the command, but it was nice to have a good loud yell.

'Over now,' was the next order from O.W., an order which was repeated by the boys. The whole school, which took up fifty or sixty yards of road, turned left. They then surged across as one man, the whole operation being over in a matter of seconds. It was not the way that Ann expected

71

a party of boys to be led across the road, but it was certainly effective.

'An advance in line abreast,' remarked Matron to her. 'A good manoeuvre and well executed. A thousand boys could have crossed in exactly the same time.'

'All right as long as a runaway bus doesn't appear. The whole school would be wiped out by it, instead of a neat cross-section,' said Ann.

'We don't have such things in these parts, we make an engineering job of their brakes.'

At the churchyard gate, the choir and servers peeled off from the main body, proceeding unescorted to the vestry door.

'Fall out the Roman Catholics,' muttered Matron to herself. It was the order which she had given so many times during her naval career, and it suited exactly her present mood.

The school then filed in, each boy removing his scarlet cap as he entered the porch. Each boy, that is to say, except little Baker. He was determined to produce a genuflection of such remarkable devoutness that much concentration was required, and he forgot to remove his cap altogether.

'Off caps,' called out Matron with a tone of authority, and there was another call from a respectably dressed publican who was sitting near the aisle.

'Take your 'at off in the 'ouse of God,' said Jack Wright. During his very early days in the Navy, a petty officer had given him this command, and he had never forgotten it. He felt that he was called upon to employ it now, in order to back up Matron. The result was unforeseen. Young Baker removed the offending article, turned towards Jack and performed in his direction the bending of the knee which should have been directed eastwards. Although the offering was several points abaft the Almighty's beam, there can be no doubt that it was accepted in the same spirit with which it was given.

A rather anaemic bell was ringing, which gave the opportunity to Matron to whisper to Ann.

'Listen to that,' she said. 'We've a fine peal of eight bells. We used to ring them years ago, I rang the tenor bell, but we can't raise a team now.'

'What a pity,' said Ann. 'I've done a bit of change-ringing myself.'

Matron looked at Ann's forearm approvingly, and had immediate thoughts of starting up the local bell-ringers again. The trouble had always been that the majority of them insisted that they were in a muck sweat after their labours, and retired across the road to the Green Dragon for liquid refreshment without going through the formality of attending what to them was unimportant, the service whose impending start they were proclaiming. Matron had a sneaking feeling that Father Mirfield would not be sympathetic to this custom, and likewise that, for once, his opinion might be correct.

'See that side chapel to starboard?' she continued. 'Used to be the vestry, but one altar wasn't good enough for Father Mirfield.'

'It's quite usual to have a side chapel,' said Ann, 'for weekday celebrations, you know.'

Matron made a disapproving noise, such as Mrs Proudie would have made had the Dean of Barchester started such nonsense.

'Well, just look at that,' she said, pointing to a red lamp which was hanging there.

'Yes,' said Ann, 'I don't think it means very much. The white light over the altar is for the reserved sacrament.'

'But that light's red. Whoever heard of a red light on the starboard side? Most confusing, ought to be green, you know.'

Before she got onto the white light, over which she held equally strong views, the choir advanced up the aisle. To

73

the fore were the head chorister, Golightly, and a village youth. The latter's voice had recently broken, and he was expected to open and shut his mouth without actually making any noise. He was being trained for a job with a candle, but was slow to learn and had already very nearly singed off one side of the duty MC's moustache. Knowing that he might desert if he had nothing to do, Father Mirfield had insisted that he should play this silent part in the choir until ready for other duties. In descending order of musical merit came the rest, with a small tail of probationers, in cassocks but as yet unrobed. The boys were plastered with medals, some of them at the end of red and others of blue ribbons. Flip Flap considered that if her choir was affiliated to the Royal School of Church Music, then everyone should know of it.

There was a gap, and the choir had already reached their places when Father Mirfield and his helpers came. They were led by Hugh Williams, the thurifer, and his attendant boat boy, the smallest boy in the school. At the approach of the incense – and Hugh was an adept at making the smoke which gladdened Father Mirfield's heart – Matron took one Protestant sniff.

'A whole destroyer flotilla couldn't do better,' she said, and clapped a large handkerchief ostentatiously in front of her nose.

Next came the crucifer, flanked by two senior boys bearing candles. He was the villager who had not supported Jack during his game of shove ha'penny with Hugh, and he was not forgiven.

'Hold it straight,' said Jack out of the corner of his mouth.

'What?' said the enemy.

'T'cross, you fool,' said Jack.

'Mind your own bloody business,' retorted the official, to the huge delight of his acolytes.

He was followed by a posse of four small candle-bearers,

hedging in the two MCs. This duty was shared by Tony, who had always had high church leanings, and the local butcher. The last-named gentleman, on duty this Sunday, had once been in the RAF, and was inordinately proud of the handlebars on his upper lip which the non-performing member of the choir had so nearly ruined. Purely on account of his appearance, he was judged by the populace to be the more spectacular of the two MCs. Father Mirfield brought up the rear, his shrewd old eyes noticing the absence of one or two of the faithful, as he walked up the aisle. He was gratified, however, to discover at one moment that he was passing between the Scylla of Jack Wright and the Charybdis of Miss Horatia Blake. Both of them were convinced that they had attracted an ecclesiastical wink, but he maintained afterwards that he was merely blinking in surprise at their unexpected presence.

Nothing untoward occurred before the final hymn, the whole service going according to plan. The sermon was very short, only ten minutes, and yet Father Mirfield had something to say to all his congregation. On one occasion, there was joyous laughter from young and old alike. O.W. did not really approve of such frivolity from the pulpit, preferring a peaceful drone so that he could quietly doze, but Father Mirfield was quite prepared to say anything which would show that his flock was awake. There had, in fact, been occasions in the past when his black congregation had been rolling in the aisle, his ex-parishioners in far-off Maquemique greatly enjoying a good laugh.

The fiasco of the last hymn was all Flip Flap's fault. To ordinary folk, there are some musicians who seem asses, and Flip Flap was a prize ass in her own right, as well as being a musician. First of all, she decided to try out a new tune to an old favourite, always a risky thing to do. Whilst an organist likes to change to something soulful, musical and very probably Welsh, the ordinary layman prefers the old tonsil-revealing shout. Secondly, and this is where she really made chaos inevitable, she pledged the choir to secrecy. The substitution was to be a complete surprise, and actually Mike was the only other adult in on the secret.

Mike had a pleasant tenor voice, much needed to offset the basso profundo of the local postman, and he sat behind the choir, together with half a dozen others. Also from the school were Topsy and Tony when not on MC duty, but the most outstanding singer was the milkman, whose surprising range veered from the wholly masculine to a wavering falsetto castrato. They did not robe, but they sang lustily and occasionally went to choir practice. Alone of these worthies, Mike had attended the secret session when the fatal tune was rehearsed, and he was the only person who could have appreciated that the situation was fraught with disaster. Boys do not think much about the results of their actions, and Flip Flap seldom thought at all. Mike, however, would have guessed the result, had he known that 'Hymn 385' in *The English Hymnal* – 'Father, hear the prayer we offer' – sung to the tune 'Sussex' was Old Willerby's favourite, and regarded by him as 'The Wintergreen Hymn'.

Quite unaware of the effect which it was producing, Flip Flap played through the tune. The choir looked both superior and smug, for they knew that they would have the first two verses to themselves whilst the congregation orientated itself from the ancient to the modern. The boys and villagers showed surprise, a surprise tinged with genuine regret. The choir did sometimes do the dirty on them, and this was one of those occasions. But it was upon the faces of the staff, Ken and Matron and, most of all, O.W. himself, that distaste was really marked.

'The wrong ruddy tune,' muttered Ken, and he shut his book with a bang. This sort of thing was too bad; here was a hymn all about mountains, and he was dashed if he was going to sing it to a tune which appeared to have been written by some moron who had never seen one.

Matron just couldn't believe her ears. To her, it was like some experienced rating heaving the lead, and then calling out the depths in the metric system. She gritted her teeth, preparing to do what she could but reconciled to the fact that an engineering job was utterly impossible.

Old Willerby adopted a different attitude. He sang both loudly and well, and he had the full music edition open ready at the place.

'I'll teach her,' he said to himself, and he ignored the lead which both organ and choir were giving him. 'Sussex' was the proper tune for this hymn, and 'Sussex' he sang.

Throughout the first verse, there was a stunned silence from the rest of the congregation, but the choir was going very nicely to Flip Flap's tune. It seemed unlikely that O.W. would survive all four verses, and Jack Wright was mentally putting his money on the choir, when treachery amongst their own ranks turned the tables on them. That non-singing chorister, the village lad with a broken voice and not much brain, was the cause of their downfall. All through the service, he had obeyed instructions to the letter, and no sound had come from his constantly moving lips. Unfortunately for the choir, the excitement of the contest was now too much for him, and he plunged into the second verse with gay abandon.

'Not for ever in the green pastures,' he wheezed and croaked, 'do we ask our way to be.'

The rhythm and the verse were lost amongst those untuneful green pastures, and even the more experienced stopped in mid-note to listen. The day might yet have been saved, for Golightly's stern eye and his neighbour's kick on the ankle both got through to the offender – but the milkman behind them put paid to their endeavours. Hearing the trebles falter, he cast aside all signs of manhood.

'But the steep and rugged pathway,' he sang in his most devastating falsetto, 'may we tread rejoicingly.'

The choir collapsed into hopeless laughter, and Matron came in heavily on O.W.'s side. It was the Nelson Touch all right, the rest of the congregation followed her lead, and it didn't matter a tinker's curse what Flip Flap was doing on the organ, for she was submerged. Led by Mike and Tony, the choir gradually pulled itself together, and by the last verse was singing the 'proper tune' with some of its lost vigour. Flip Flap had much to say on the matter, but could find little comfort from her listeners.

There were ten bodies for Ken's climbing test that afternoon, seven boys and the three members of the staff. Apart from the two tiddlers and the great Duffield, a quartet of Common Entrance formers, all of whom have been mentioned before, lent tone to the party. Macpherson, who was large, and Smythe, who was small, were games players; Wilkinson, who was thin, and Golightly, who was fat, were not. Golightly was the least likely to be efficient, but he possessed a tenacity of purpose which did much to offset his physical defects. Aided by his friend Macpherson, he had put in a lot of practice on the sly, and the climb held no terrors for him.

'Come on, Golly,' said Macpherson, as they prepared for the ascent. 'Sir's going to hold the end of the rope, so it doesn't matter if you do slip.'

'OK, Mac, but I don't think I'll need the rope.'

'It'll break with your weight, Golly,' put in Wilkinson a little unkindly, 'but you'll bounce all right.'

'Now then, Wilks. Just because I'm not skinny like you, you needn't talk like that.'

'Just stop arguing,' said Ken, 'Do as you're told, and you won't be testing the rope.'

'Yes, sir. Let's get cracking,' said Macpherson.

The climb onto the junior changing-room roof presented

no problems. It was close to the playground, and there was hardly a boy in the school who hadn't been up there at one time or another after a lost ball. It wasn't allowed, of course, but that made it all the more attractive. Even Golightly made short work of it, though Duffield criticised his technique. The traverse to the boot-hole had one tricky section, but Ken was there, ready to support the weak and encourage the faint-hearted. That his assistance was required in neither capacity augured well for the crux of the climb, a descent through the skylight into the boot-hole. A slight overhang had to be negotiated before the simple descent down the lockers could begin. The party roped up for this, and Ken was stationed below to guide erring feet. Wildly swinging legs, however, found footholds in the lockers quite safely, and no one required his help.

'Please, sir,' said Anderson. 'That was smashing. Will we have anything like this in the Lake District?'

'Nothing so difficult,' answered Ken quite truthfully.

'Oh, that's a swizz, sir.'

'Ah,' broke in the learned Duffield,' but weather conditions won't be so good, and the rock face will be more exposed.'

He spoke pontifically, and with the authority of one who had at least scaled successfully the north face of the Eiger. It was certainly more exposed when they reached the pitch onto the lab roof. There were some twenty feet of climbing, so anyone with no head for heights would have suffered acutely. Fortunately, there were no green faces, and the trek over to the kitchen roof followed without mishap. The final pitch down the drainpipe was straightforward, as there were admirable handholds. Ken sent Ann down first.

'You might like to traverse along that ledge over the window,' he said. 'It's an interesting variation.'

Its classification was probably no higher than 'moderate', and Ann made it look easy, so easy that Golightly, who was following, thought that he would try the same route. He hadn't actually been told to use the direct route down the drainpipe, so he started off along the ledge at the rate of knots.

'I think I'd go straight down,' said Ken rather too late – and he did.

Golightly was traversing magnificently, but he slipped at the crucial moment. Gently gyrating, he swung across the kitchen window on the end of the rope.

'Hello, Mrs Emmerson,' he said conversationally to the cook, who was washing up.

To see a stout figure swinging past your nose when you are not expecting it is unnerving, to say the least, and Mrs Emmerson was always liable to panic. She uttered a loud scream, and dropped the plate which she was holding with a crash. This piercing yell, and the attendant sound of breakage, rather shattered those up above, who could see little of what was happening.

'My God,' said Ken to Mike, 'if I've killed him, the trip's off!'

He was reassured to see Ann in fits of laughter, and everyone soon knew what had happened.

'Right, I'm pulling him up again for another shot. If he puts his foot through the window, he's not coming with us,' said Ken.

Hand over hand, the fallen warrior was pulled up, and he arrived at the top little the worse for wear.

'That illustrates the value of the three-point hold,' lectured Duffield. 'If you'd been climbing properly, Golly, that would never have happened.'

'You'd better try it, and show us how it ought to be done,' said Mike.

'A splendid idea. We'll have you all down, and then you can watch,' said Ken. 'You go down the drainpipe this time, Golightly. After Mr Thornton, please, and he can show you where to put your clumsy great feet.'

This time, he descended more gracefully, the services of the rope not being required, and soon all but Ken and Duffield had reached the ground.

'Now then, Tensing,' said Ken. 'Let's see that technique of yours.'

Duffield started off slowly but confidently. Three-point hold notwithstanding, poor Mrs Emmerson had another shock, and broke another plate. Even on the end of the rope, Duffield managed to preserve his dignity, and one felt that his downfall was due to circumstances quite beyond his control.

6

Half-term fever had been fuelled a good week before the holiday began by O.W.'s noisy visits to each form in turn in order to compile lists of boys not going by train. This dated back to the days when only a handful were collected by car. For many years now, he would have saved himself a lot of writing by taking down the names of those who were going by train, but routine could not be shattered. He managed to disorganise the school for half an hour in order to fill three sheets of paper when all that he really needed was three names.

By the last day of October, the excitement had reached new heights, for half-term started on the morrow. Before leaving for home, however, the school had to attend chapel, for Father Mirfield would never permit his flock to slip from his clutches without a service on All Saints' Day.

The packing off of seventy-eight small boys, complete with bags and baggage, was quite an undertaking, and both Matron and Ann were kept hard at it.

'What will you be doing, Horatia?' asked Ann, as they worked together in Matapan.

'Just look at Golightly's drawer. He'll have to make that shipshape before he goes ashore,' remarked Matron. 'What was that you said?'

'Are you doing anything exciting this weekend?'

'Oh, nothing much, my dear. I'm getting old, you know.'

Thereupon, she gave a catalogue of furious activity, which included the Saturday afternoon with Colonel Dalton's basset hounds, followed in the evening by a big Wren reunion, a

82

reunion which she herself had organised. She made it quite clear that she would be the chief, if not the only, speaker.

'I always regard half-term as a make and mend, you know. I catch up on all the things which I can't do when the boys are around.'

'When do you want me back on Monday?' Ann asked.

'Oh, there's not much to do. I shall be about during the dog watches, so your shore leave can last until the boys are due to turn in – but don't you be adrift.'

'What would the punishment be?'

'A day's pay and a day's leave,' came out with no hesitation. At defaulters in the Wrens, that punishment had been a great standby for petty misdemeanours.

'Oh, I couldn't afford that. I'll be back on board in time.'

'That's good. You're going to York, I hear.'

'Yes, Mike and I are staying at the Youth Hostel. There's plenty to see in York.'

'Not a bad spot, but I prefer somewhere nearer the sea. Now good old Pompey, there's a town for you.'

'Is there much to see there?'

'Why, yes. What a question to ask. There's the naval barracks – and *Victory* in the dockyard. What more do you want?'

It was obvious that, in Matron's eyes, these two attractions far outweighed anything that York could produce, so Ann did not pursue the matter further. Instead, she reverted to Golightly's drawer, and said innocently:

'No wonder Golightly can never find anything. Have you a naval term to describe that drawer?'

'Don't you worry. I'll sort him out. Naval term? Yes, it's a nest of bastards, a proper nest of bastards.'

So it was true then. Ann had been told of the phrase, by Macpherson as a matter of fact, but she wanted to hear the words from the oracle herself.

Mercifully, next day's service was short, and by ten o'clock the last red cap, with green dragon thereon, had disappeared. Its owner had either been scooped up by parental car, or else been ferried by Ken to train or bus in Elmet. Mike and Ann had intended starting off later by the local bus, but Matron offered them a lift into Elmet in what was irreverently called the Admiral's barge. It was a Mini, painted battleship grey, and appeared to have but three speeds – full ahead, full astern and stop. Matron adopted the naval procedure, and insisted on being last in and first out on the assumption that she was always the senior officer present.

The journey to Elmet was not entirely uneventful, and one itinerant cow will suffer psychologically for the rest of its life, but the *pièce de résistance* was actually in Elmet. A stationary bus drew out in front of the Admiral's barge without sufficient indication of its intentions to satisfy the commanding officer. With a blast of her horn, certainly no standard fitting since it sounded more like the siren of some mighty man-of-war, Matron demonstrated her displeasure. She took up station astern, and bided her time. At the next stop, she drew up alongside. She leant over Mike, who was sitting beside her, before delivering a few winged words.

'You're not fit to drive a perambulator,' she boomed, and was well on her way before the discomfited driver could think up a suitable reply.

'Have a good time,' she said later to Ann and Mike, 'and mind that you behave yourselves.'

They were all three standing outside the Five Bells, which Matron had obviously chosen for its nautical name rather than its repute as a stylish port of call. She had downed three tots of rum, whilst they had been content with milder fare, had discovered that a postman sipping his pint was an ex-stoker, and had discoursed learnedly on superheated steam to his great delight. Now she was pushing them off on their own, and Mike quite expected her to ask him if he had a clean handkerchief before finally saying goodbye.

They went to the bus station, and embarked on the York bus. Matron had so fiercely denounced hitchhiking that they did not dare to employ that means of transport. With her in the vicinity, it was simply not worth risking. It was an hour's journey to York, and lunchtime when eventually they arrived at Rougier Street.

'I'm a bit peckish,' said Mike. 'I wonder if that pub over there can give us a bite, What a curious name for a pub – the Pageant.'

He pointed towards an imposing edifice on the corner, complete with revolving door.

'Pageant,' said Ann, her interest in history momentarily exceeding her hunger, 'now that strikes a chord. The old mystery plays were originally acted on carts, called pageants, and that corner must be one of the places where they paused to act them.'

'Very interesting, I'm sure, but it doesn't really get our meal much further along.'

'I knew you'd be impressed. Well, I've seen enough of the inside of licensed premises for the moment. And anyway, I'm all for something solid to eat. There's sure to be a Chinese restaurant within reach.'

Sure enough, a walk into Micklegate produced one, and they had a remarkably good meal at very moderate cost.

'Damned clever, these Chinese,' said Mike. 'We've never had a dud meal yet at one of their establishments.'

'It could be that we're always so darned hungry.'

'I know, we always are, but surely we'd notice it if the food wasn't good.'

After their meal, they walked over Ouse Bridge, crossing the road with infinite difficulty, to look upstream towards the Guildhall. The sun was shining brightly, and the scene was entrancing.

'The Romans had a bridge up there somewhere,' said Ann. 'A pity there's none of it left.'

'For the pigs to cross, I suppose.'

'Pigs? What on earth are you talking about?'

'York ham, of course. You'd need the pigs.'

An elderly workman was quite surprised when he saw the girl in front of him place a well-aimed kick on her boyfriend's backside. In his courting days, that sort of thing simply didn't happen, or if it did he'd forgotten all about it.

Once over the bridge, Mike noticed the figure of a white cat, perched high up on the sill of a blocked-in window.

'Do look,' he said. 'Statue of a Roman cat – Egyptian influence, no doubt. I don't mind betting that the average citizen of York doesn't know it's there.'

But that is where he was wrong. He stopped as he pointed, and the workman bumped into him.

'Sorry, lad,' he said. 'Looking at t'cat, weren't you?'

'Yes. What's it doing there?'

'Couldn't say, lad, but it's been there a long time. And there's a dog on t'wall next door.'

'So there is,' said Ann, 'but it looks more like a black cat.'

'Nay, love, it's a dog.'

'Much more like a cat,' said Ann, sticking to her guns.

A lengthy inspection from below produced no clear-cut decision, but quite a crowd gathered round them. Cat or dog, there it was attached to the wall, and some twenty citizens of York continued the argument long after Mike and Ann had walked quietly away.

'It's a bloody cat,' a large and belligerent gentleman was proclaiming to the assembled company as they retreated.

'But it's a dog, always has been,' countered their friend the workman.

'Of course it's a bloody cat,' shouted the large gentleman and, whether his cause was just or not, many of those nearest to him agreed with him.

'He's right, you know,' said Ann to Mike. 'It is a bloody cat.'

'Well, whatever it is, it's been there a long time. Let's go and find the Minster while the sun is shining. You can tell me all about the glass.'

They walked up High Ousegate and across Parliament Street into Pavement.

'How very odd,' said Mike. 'Half these streets seem to be "gates", and here's a road which is all "pavement".'

They passed one narrow entrance on the left without really noticing it, and took the second, as it seemed to lead in the general direction of the Minster.

'Oh, no, I don't believe that one,' suddenly exclaimed Mike, as he pointed at a street name. 'It can't really be Whip-ma-whop-ma-gate – hallucination probably.'

'It isn't, it's perfectly true. I can't remember who it was that got whipped and whopped here, either the hounds of Hungate or the felons of the locality.'

'But the street isn't much longer than the sign. Let's see where this alleyway leads.'

He plunged down a little snicket to the left, with Ann close on his heels, and they came out into York's most famous thoroughfare, the Shambles. They walked up it towards the Minster, both of them being suitably impressed by the mediaeval houses, especially the two whose upper storeys bulged outwards, seemingly determined to cut off completely the narrow thread of sky which separated them. They paused at a shop to buy a plan of the city, a shop so crammed with books that its proprietor appeared utterly hemmed in.

'I'd love to work in a shop like that,' said Ann, as they left it. 'It would be so exciting delving down to find out what treasures lurked in the lower strata.'

In a very few minutes, they reached the south door of the Minster, but Ann declared that she always liked to walk round the outside of a church before studying the interior. She was about to turn right, but Mike stopped her.

'You don't know the first thing about churches,' he said. 'Never walk round one in an anticlockwise direction. That's widdershins, and extremely dangerous.'

'Dangerous? Why?'

'I'm not absolutely sure, something to do with witches, I think.'

'Oh, I might be whipped and whopped by them, and I should hate that. Left it is then, and I hope that we can get round.'

They passed between the ancient church of St Michael le Belfry and the Minster.

'That seems a soppy place for a church,' said Mike, pointing at St Michael's. 'Surely the local inhabitants could always pop into the Minster for a quick prayer.'

'It may look a bit silly now, but there must be some reason. How do you know there wasn't a wall between them at one time?'

'Was there? Was the Minster a monastery?'

'I don't really know – I was just trying to give you an explanation to keep you quiet.'

'Well, I'm quite sure that some mediaeval dean preached such ghastly sermons that a rival concern was put up next door. Oh, do look at that, Ann.'

They had passed the end of the church, and a hotel came into view. Above the door was a large sign, which stated that, in 1570, Guy Fawkes had been born there.

'I knew he was a York man,' said Ann. 'He was educated at St Peter's School, and that's on our way to the hostel, I think.'

'I wonder how they celebrate the fifth of November. Do you think they put a model of the Houses of Parliament on their bonfire?'

'You'd better pay a call on them and ask the headmaster.'

If you introduced yourself as a fellow schoolmaster, I'm sure he'd answer your query.'

By this time, they had walked past the west front, and had passed through a gate into the Dean's Park. They admired from a distance the lovely early English library, and, passing through another gate, they paused in front of the Treasurer's House.

'What do you think of that?' asked Ann. 'Isn't it a beautiful setting?'

'It's perfect,' said Mike. 'York would be worth a visit just to see that.'

They looked at the Chapter House, with its steep roof, and soon they were at the east end, gazing up at the colossal window.

'That's all ancient glass,' said Ann, 'over five hundred and fifty years old.'

'It doesn't look anything wonderful. Anyway, how do you know how old it is?'

'That's just for protection. The old stuff is inside. The glass was put in by a certain John Thornton, between 1405 and 1408.'

'Do you know, I think you're pulling my leg.'

'No, I'm not, Mike. The indenture between the Dean and Chapter of York and John Thornton still exists. And I believe the date's on the window somewhere.'

They walked round to their starting point at the south door. Very ancient and solid it was, but Mike gave a good shove, and they were in.

As can be guessed, Ann's hobby was ancient glass. She had visited the early glories of Canterbury Cathedral and the later wonders of Fairford Church, in Gloucestershire. She was familiar with the technical terms – cartoons and pot metal and yellow stain, and she knew exactly for what purpose a grozing iron was kept. It can therefore be imagined that Mike was in for a pretty intensive lecture on the subject, for York Minster must contain very nearly as much ancient glass in its many windows as the rest of the churches of England put together. To Mike, a piece of glass was just a piece of glass, and it is to be feared that he found the afternoon's entertainment a little overpowering, as they progressed from the geometrical wizardry of the patterns in the *Five Sisters* to the picture windows of the nave. Some of these were delightfully clear, whilst others told stories which were difficult to unravel, in spite of the many years of loving care which had been lavished on their restoration.

After what seemed rather a long time to Mike, and but the twinkling of an eye to Ann, they paused before the vastness and the perfection of the great East Window.

'Look at it,' exclaimed Ann. 'It's as big as a tennis court, and there are nearly a hundred and fifty different panels. No wonder it took three years to complete.'

'I have to admit that I'm impressed. It's very big and very beautiful – but what's it all about?'

'The top three rows are Old Testament scenes, and the rest is the Revelation of St John. Oh, I do wish I had some binoculars with me.'

Her wish was answered, for an old gentleman who was standing by took pity on her. He too was an enthusiast, and he possessed the proper equipment.

'Would you care to share these with me, my dear?' he said. 'Let's sit down here, and study the window together.'

Within seconds, they were immersed. The old gentleman read out the subject matter of a row and Ann looked. Ann took the booklet from him and read out, while the old gentleman gazed upwards. The panels were a yard across and even with the naked eye Mike could spot the very orange-coloured apples in the Garden of Eden and a placid looking St John sitting in a cauldron of oil before his journey to the island of Patmos. All the same, he felt a little left out. He looked up at the window – as big as a tennis court, Ann had said – and pictured John the Divine plucking apples from the branches of the Tree of Knowledge of Good and Evil, and serving them into the Sea of Glass with unbelievable accuracy. After a couple of love games, Mike decided to wander, as he was unlikely to get much sense out of Ann whilst she was within reach of the binoculars. To her excited exclamations that she could see a date in one of the tracery lights, he sauntered into the south choir aisle. There he paused in front of an imposing monument, whose date, MDCV, would have been an admirable test in Roman numerals for his pupils. The sculptors of Shakespeare's day had certainly lost the grace of those who executed the figures of crusaders and their ladies on earlier tombs. Those noble effigies, at least, did look comfortable, but this poor fellow had been leaning on one elbow for three hundred and fifty years – and he looked as if he was feeling it acutely. His feet, moreover, were hanging in mid-air in a most unsatisfactory manner. The sculptors of earlier times got over the difficulty by permitting their subjects to rest their feet on lions or dogs, but poor old Archbishop Hutton's feet had no such comforting support.

'*Epitaphum Matthaei Huttoni celeberrimi Archiepiscopi Eboracensis...*' read Mike. He thought that possibly the third form might see some use for Latin if they were confronted with something of this sort, rather than the uninspiring sentences of the textbook then in use at Wintergreen. Who the blazes was Archbishop Hutton anyway? He hadn't lost his head, like Scrope, or died in the expectation of losing it, like Cardinal Wolsey. These were the only Archbishops of York that Mike could recall at the moment, and he was interrupted in his musings by Ann and her escort.

'We can't see the third row of the Old Testament panels,' said Ann sadly.

'Why not? Is it getting too dark?'

'No, they're completely hidden by a miserable balcony affair.'

'That's the tennis net,' said Mike, to the mystification of both Ann and the old gentleman.

'That balcony supports the window,' said the old gentleman. 'It isn't there just to obstruct the view.'

'It seems a waste of time and energy to put in panels where nobody can see them,' said Mike.

'Oh, I think that John Thornton designed the window for the glory of God,' continued the old gentleman. 'He probably didn't mind all that much that the general public's view was obscured.'

'I'm not so sure about that, sir,' said Mike. 'I bet there was a terrible scene when it was discovered that the panels were hidden. Surely, artistic temperament ran just as wild in those days, and John Thornton probably sued the Dean and Chapter for ancient lights or damages or something.'

'There is no record of such an event,' said the old gentleman drily. 'Anyway, by peering through the gateway in the choir screen we can see them splendidly.'

Mike accompanied them, and was impressed by the ancient stone screen, with its row of Kings of England, starting with William the Conqueror and finishing at Henry the Sixth.

'There's Henry the Fourth,' said the old gentleman, pointing at one of the later kings. 'He was responsible for cutting off Scrope's head, you know. It wasn't a popular move at all up here, so they canonised the Archbishop, and painted Henry's face black.'

'It does look a bit shadowy under his chin,' said Ann.

'Perhaps, but most of the paint's worn off. The Clerk of the Works ought to come round with his pot and touch him up,' said Mike.

'Well, the screen was put up in the late fourteen-hundreds, and I don't suppose that later embellishments of that nature would be encouraged,' said the old gentleman.

'I'm sorry Henry the Eighth's not on. If they liked Wolsey, they'd have done something interesting to him.'

'You prize nit,' said Ann. 'How on earth could he be on it?'

'Screen's not wide enough, I suppose.'

'No, you idiot. I doubt if Henry the Eighth was born when the screen was finished.'

'Let's see. Richard the Third – 1483, Henry the Seventh – 1485, Henry the Eighth – 1509. Yes, I suppose there's something in what you say…' But Mike was left muttering the dates to himself, for Ann and her friend were working steadily along the line of panels now revealed to them. Starting with Moses in the bulrushes, they dealt briefly with his adult life and finished with three catastrophes, the death of Samson, David and Goliath and Absalom in the tree.

By the time that they had examined the window, the light was failing, and vergers were closing in on them in order to clear the decks for evensong. The old gentleman allowed himself to be swept away by them, but Mike and Ann decided to stay. They were ushered into two of the prebendal stalls, marked 'Apesthorpe' and 'Dunnington' respectively.

'What happens if the rightful owners turn up un-expectedly?' whispered Mike. 'If I were Prebendary of Apesthorpe, I'd take a very poor view of the occupation of my private stall by a female.'

'And what about Canon Dunnington? If he should arrive now, he'd be entitled to sling you out.'

Fortunately, no such scene took place, and the temporary stall-holders were able to enjoy the service in peace.

It was nearly dark when they left the Minster, and walked through Bootham Bar on their way to the hostel. After the fine Georgian houses of Bootham, they approached a graceful modern footbridge across the road, with some seemingly ancient buildings on the left.

'These must belong to St Peter's School,' said Ann,

pointing in the direction of the buildings. 'I wonder what sort of a place it is.'

'I've never met anyone connected with it,' said Mike. 'Guy Fawkes was a little before my time. It's a very old public school, but it hasn't been in the top twenty for about a thousand years, I should say.'

'The buildings look imitation Gothic, like the Houses of Parliament, but I do like that bridge.'

'Let's cross the road by it. Do you think it's school property?'

'I don't know – there's nothing to tell us. We'd better thank the Board of Governors, just in case.'

'Distinguished Gentlemen of the Board,' said Mike, as they reached the other side, 'our united thanks to you for the use of your magnificent bridge. If it's not yours, just forget it.'

Two small boys in shorts, and with dark blue caps perched conspicuously on their heads, looked startled. The white crossed keys upon the caps proclaimed that, in all probability, they had something to do with St Peter, and Mike engaged them in conversation.

'Are you at St Peter's?' he asked.

'No, sir, we're Olavites,' replied one of them.

'And what are they when they're at home?'

'We're at St Olave's, sir. The Peterites are at St Peter's.'

'Do you mean that St Olave's is the prep school for St Peter's?'

'Yes, sir,' replied the other, 'my brother's a Peterite.'

'And do all of you go on up to St Peter's?'

'Oh yes, sir.'

'And do you all have to pass the Common Entrance?'

'What's that, sir?' they asked in chorus.

'From that, it's obvious that you don't. I think you're lucky,' said Mike.

Now the Common Entrance examination is a kind of

fetish at a normal preparatory school, something to be
treated with semi-religious awe. Like the eleven-plus, its state
counterpart, it is not now considered with quite the respect
that it used to be, but it is a very necessary hurdle for the
thirteen-year-old prep school boy. And here was a fortunate
school which could bypass the whole thing. Provided that
he was not half-witted and of undesirable character, it
seemed that an Olavite was educationally secure. Old Willerby
wouldn't like this idea, but it seemed sound education to
Mike. This ancient foundation had gone all comprehensive
well ahead of its time. From the age of eight until a boy
left school for good, his course of studies could be planned.
There would be a break between junior and senior schools,
it is true, but this would not be the major upheaval to which
the Wintergreen boys were subjected when they went on
to their public schools.

'We did have an entrance exam before we came to St
Olave's,' volunteered one of the boys.

'I didn't really pass,' said the other, 'but I got in all right.'

'And how many of you are there?'

'Two hundred and twenty,' said one boy.

'More like two hundred and forty, sir,' said the other.
'Here's the school list.'

He pulled a brightly covered booklet from his pocket, a
booklet which had already done yeoman service, and
thumbed the pages.

'Two hundred and thirty-seven, sir,' he said triumphantly.
'You're wrong, Smudge.'

'My word, you're thick on the ground,' said Mike.

'Is Smudge your real name?' asked Ann, turning to the
more silent one.

'Oh no, but you should see his exercise books,' said
Smudge's friend.

'Watch it,' said Smudge, 'or I shan't help you with your
maths prep.'

After a few more minutes of this interesting conversation, the Olavites saw a bus approaching.

'We must fly, or we'll miss the bus,' they shouted. They charged across the bridge, but in their flight remembered to raise their caps politely.

'Those were two very nice lads,' said Ann. 'They'd plenty to say for themselves all right.'

'Yes. I must find out rather more about the school. Two hundred and forty's far too big though.'

The Wintergreen influence had definitely impressed itself on him. A mere six weeks ago, mention of that number would not have affected Mike either way, and now he was championing the smaller school. Incidentally, he was interested to find out later that St Olave's had once been in the Association of Preparatory Schools, but had fallen by the wayside. Mike felt then that, whatever had been the cause of the trouble, there was little wrong with the boys.

Mike and Ann had booked their evening meal at the hostel and, as it was at six o'clock, they had plenty of time after it to sample the nightlife of York. A knowledgeable fellow hosteller recommended the theatre and the first pub on the left on their way there. His advice was taken, and an enjoyable evening followed.

Saturday started damp and foggy, very different weather from the sunshine of their first day. It was obviously a morning for the Castle Museum, the warden had told them, and there they went, albeit somewhat reluctantly.

'Museums aren't my cup of tea at all,' said Mike. 'I can't think why you're dragging me there.'

'I have to be in the mood too. Would you like to do a tour of the York churches instead? There's some good glass in many of them.'

'It can stay there,' said Mike, and he chose the lesser of two evils.

He needn't have worried at all, for the Castle Museum

is something to which the most unenthusiastic of visitors can take no exception. Mike thoroughly enjoyed it, and it was lunchtime before they had explored both museum buildings and Clifford's Tower, the only remaining part of the ancient castle. The fog had lifted and a rather watery sun broke through. When they had had their lunch, Ann and Mike parted, the former determined to do the churches of York and the latter to watch a game of some kind. He would have liked to follow the fortunes of York City, which was going through one of its better phases and had climbed well into the top half of the fourth division, but there was no match that afternoon. He toyed with the idea of rugby league, and then thought that perhaps St Peter's or St Olave's might have a home match.

Retracing his steps, he reached the footbridge, and was extremely lucky to run into the same two Olavites to whom he had spoken the night before. They took him under their wing, leading him down a lane and through an archway to the first fifteen field. St Peter's were playing, and the exceptional merits of the home team were expounded at great length by Smudge and his pal. No fewer than eleven Old Olavites were in the team which, according to their calculations, made it more or less invincible. St Peter's certainly won that afternoon, and Mike was struck by the keenness of the spectators, whose cheers made the welkin ring. This was something which he had not experienced at his school, where there was seldom more than a handful of supporters to encourage the first eleven.

After the match, Mike was escorted round the school, by which time darkness was falling, and he had not long to wait before the doors of the hostel were opened to him. The evening was spent in the hostel, where a good time was had by all.

Sunday morning was spent mainly in the Minster, for they attended morning prayer and then stayed on for the sung Eucharist. The afternoon was devoted to a walk round the city walls. Mike was prepared to argue that he was not being well-treated when they came to a big gap in the defences, and was hardly mollified by Ann's explanation that an impenetrable morass made walls there unnecessary.

'You told me that the walls were complete,' he insisted, 'and don't tell me that this soppy little river could have stopped a determined invader.'

'It was a marsh in the Middle Ages. Haven't you ever heard of drainage?'

Later, the hospitable doors of St Helen's beckoned them in to a hearty service. Here was a city church which seemed to be alive. After the service and a meal, the two of them had letters to write. The Sunday letter home was a ritual to which they had been introduced rather late in life, but nobody could be at Wintergreen for just one Sunday without realising its importance. It is by no means certain that a boarder in a preparatory school turns into a better letter writer than a day boy elsewhere, but no one can say that he doesn't get more practice.

Monday dawned fair, and they had a further prowl round the city, this time paying particular attention to those Roman features which were readily accessible to the public. Even Mike could appreciate the rarity of so much Roman masonry above ground level. The Multangular Tower was, of course, inspected from every one of its angles, likewise the rather cheeky little piece of Roman wall in St Leonard's. It really seemed to have no business to be there after all those years.

'It's been sitting there for over fifteen hundred years,' said Mike, as they looked at it, 'and people are just passing it as if it was any old wall.'

'It saw the Sixth Legion leave,' said Ann, waxing quite poetical, 'and it will still be here after all of us are dead and forgotten.'

'Unless some builder runs up a department store here, and puts a bulldozer at it before anyone can protest.'

Then began the journey back to Wintergreen. Considering themselves to be beyond the effective range of Matron's radar screen, they hitchhiked shamelessly and successfully, though nothing as interesting as Dalton's purple van was going their way. Ann, it is pleasing to report, was not adrift.

7

'And finally, Mike, do what you can to keep O.W. away from the fireworks; he's bloody dangerous.'

These words completed Mike's briefing. He had been detailed by Tony to assist him in the lighting of the fireworks at the display on 5th November. Everything possible had been done both to make the evening a success and to reduce to a minimum the chances of a major catastrophe. An area of the playground had been cordoned off in order to keep the boys at a sporting range, Matron had turned the sick bay into a casualty clearing station and all fire-fighting appliances had been thoroughly tested. There was a chance, however, that some boy or boys might soon be suffering from second-degree burns. The best-laid plans for their safety might well be sabotaged when their headmaster was apt to cast all kinds of incendiary material in their midst with a gay abandon bordering on the insane. He was the sort of person who would hold a banger in his hand until the explosion was imminent, and then cast it where the crowd was thickest. If it went off in his hand, which did happen sometimes, he regarded it as an excellent joke. He was one of those people who bore a charmed life, for he had never damaged so much as a little finger throughout his dangerous career.

There was an even greater danger to the school than to the boys. The whole establishment could so easily go up in flames, since O.W. insisted that the fireworks should be let off from a balcony overlooking the playground, rather than at the other end of the rugger field, whither they all repaired after the fireworks to share a bonfire with the villagers.

Every member of the staff had his or her allotted panic station, though it was to be hoped that the services of at least the majority of them would not be required. With matches at the ready, Mike and Tony awaited the executive command from O.W. to begin the festivities.

'Come on, up there,' he shouted at last, 'let's have some Roman candles.'

This was the traditional order, given by him each year, and Roman candles were soon shooting their coloured balls skywards in a most satisfactory manner. Ken, the duty fire officer, noted that the wind was from the west. This would make his beloved science lab the most vulnerable part of the school, and he traced in his mind's eye the course of the hose from hydrant to seat of the expected conflagration. A few moments later, one green ball landed on the roof, and, to his infinite regret later, he transferred the result of his cogitations from the purely theoretical to the practical. The hose was already connected to the main, and he had only to run it out eastwards behind the crowd. This he did on his own, for all other eyes were turned towards the glorious pyrotechnic display from the balcony.

This year, there were far more fireworks than usual. It so happened that the smallest boy in the school, Father Mirfield's boat boy, was hereditarily suited for the job. It was he who supplied the combustible material without which the censer could not swing with such good effect. His father supplied to the general public the combustible material without which displays of this nature could not take place at all. He had presented to the school an enormous quantity of first-class fireworks from his own warehouse. These arrived after the normal supplies had been tapped, and with both Tony and Mike working flat out, it seemed that two hours would not be sufficient for the expenditure of such a vast quantity of high explosive. Actually, the show was completed in one hour dead, and responsibility for this curtailment can be laid primarily at Mike's door.

'Three big rockets together now,' said Tony, doling out to his henchman a truly magnificent trio.

Mike set them in the three bottles provided, and lit them. It wasn't really his fault that the central rocket should start its journey well off course. Owing to its prodigious weight, the centre of gravity of the rocket and launching pad was dangerously high. Perhaps it was a minute puff of wind, perhaps it was the effect of the down-blast as the powder ignited which caused the bottle to fall, but fall it did at the crucial moment.

A rocket is rather poor company in a crowd, and its effect as it sped towards the heart of it was truly devastating. Golightly's portly figure in the front rank of spectators swayed in exactly the right direction at exactly the right moment, or the missile would have scored a direct hit on his protruding solar plexus. No matador could have avoided the horns of a charging bull more gracefully. Three boys behind him cast themselves upon the ground in much the same way as their parents or their grandparents might have done, had a bomb been descending upon them during World War Two. Behind the boys was Mr Topsy Turner, complete with little attaché case. He had been stationed in the rear as a kind of liaison officer-cum-stretcher-bearer, a fact which he rather resented. He was a small man, and he had already noted with disgust that the heads of the taller boys obstructed his view of the firing platform. He was extremely partial to Catherine wheels, and he had missed the performance of a whole battery of the most expensive models.

Topsy saw two giant rockets zooming upwards, and he saw that something peculiar was happening to that section of the crowd which lay between him and the balcony. A way was carved through the crowd and, in less time than it takes to tell it, his view was no longer obscured. Homing upon his third fly button downwards was a deadly missile, apparently bent on the destruction of his matrimonial prospects. It was a terrible shock to him, for although a rocket is a delightful sight when viewed in full retreat, it is awe-inspiring when approaching one's vitals at an ever-increasing velocity. Time for Topsy stood sufficiently still for him to appreciate that to use his attaché case as a kind of armoured fig leaf was the only possible thing to do. He placed his shield in the correct position and hoped for the best.

What then happened was not, according to the one scientist on the staff, a ballistic possibility. By some quirk of fate impossible to explain, the upward movement of Topsy's attaché case deflected the rocket from its unfortunate horizontal flight to one which was practically vertical. It was not noticed until much later that, as its trajectory altered, it had completely singed off the eyebrows of the man who had reorganised its course. It sped upwards in pursuit of its two brothers, and burst with them into a thousand little stars, though naturally somewhat lower in the firmament.

From Topsy's case came a terrible roar, which was quickly recognised as a perfect reproduction of O.W. on the warpath. The mystery of the case was out; it was a tape recorder of advanced design, and was used by Topsy in his researches. Unknown to his headmasters, he could faithfully record their every word, and listen at leisure as many times as was necessary for his investigations. The rocket had done something to the mechanism, and the machine was permanently switched on to 'play'. There was nothing that Topsy could do but retreat with his plaything as quickly as possible.

Before Topsy had gone three paces, the playground was bathed in light. Hugh was stationed near the switch, and it was his duty to turn on the floodlighting, something which

103

O.W. had dreamed up after an evening visit to a local *Son et Lumière*, at the first sign of trouble. The voice which everyone heard in the darkness spelt trouble with a capital 'T', so he was perfectly justified in so doing. The result was positively eerie, for O.W. was to be seen standing near to Flip Flap in one corner, whilst his voice was being carried rapidly away towards the other by the unfortunate Topsy. Never before had O.W. been unable to make himself heard, and it was indeed poetic justice that it should have been his own voice which defeated him so completely. He stood opening and shutting his mouth like a fish out of water, whilst the volume of sound gradually diminished. By the time that distance and a couple of closed doors had damped it completely down, the brighter members of the assembled company had gathered what had happened, and their shrieks of merriment were repeated by the dumber ones, who still vaguely suspected witchcraft.

'Splendid,' shouted O.W. at last, for he liked people to enjoy themselves, 'but out with the lights, and let's get on with it. We don't want to be late for the bonfire.'

He glanced at his watch as he spoke, saw that time was speeding on and decided to go up to the balcony and lend a hand. This was something which Tony most certainly did not want, and indeed Flip Flap had been commissioned to head him off at all costs if he looked like interfering. The lights went out, and Flip Flap went boldly into action.

'Oh no, headmaster,' she started brightly. 'Tony and Mike are doing very well, and I'm sure they'll manage all right. I always say that two's company, you know – and three's a crowd. You had much better stay down here and talk to me. And you can deal with the next crisis, that's if there is one. You saw what happened to that rocket, and it could happen again. Topsy seems to have left us, and I can't quite make out what happened. His voice sounded just like yours, you know. It was very clever of him, but I can't quite think why everyone laughed so much. I wonder if anything's wrong. You just stay here, and I'll go and see if I can help him. Will that be all right, Headmaster?'

She paused for a reply, but answer came there none. This was hardly surprising, for O.W. had long since departed, and was even now in the library, outside whose windows the fireworks were being discharged.

'That rocket was a splendid idea,' he said, as he opened the door and walked onto the balcony. 'Shall we try a whole battery at them?'

'Oh, my God,' said Tony.

The system having broken down, here was big trouble for the organiser. O.W. took no notice. Tapping out his pipe, he put it in his pocket and picked up a firework at random.

'Looks a bit like a mills bomb,' he said meditatively. 'We'll light it up, Mike, and it should stir them up if we toss it into the middle of them.'

'Oh no, sir,' said Mike. 'That's part of a particularly beautiful set piece we are saving up for the end.'

'A pity,' said O.W. with a sigh, and Mike made a mental note that he would have to invent something at the end of the show to fit in with his remark, which was the first thing that had come into his head.

The display continued uninterrupted for a few more minutes, though the running of it became more difficult. Tony and Mike took it in turns to stand between O.W. and the arsenal, and in this way they felt that they had the situation well under control. How very wrong they were!

It must have been the contents of O.W.'s pipe which got in amongst the still imposing pile of unexpended fireworks; there is no other explanation. With a sudden whoosh, something powerful went off, backfiring into the library through the door which O.W. had omitted to close. With commendable speed, O.W. himself followed it.

'I'll put it out and save the books,' he called out, slamming the door behind him and locking it. He knew quite well that draughts must be excluded when dealing with a fire, and anyway he didn't want the rest of the funeral pyre exploding in after him.

'Well, I'll be damned,' said Tony. 'He's all right, Jack, he's inboard. I wonder if we can save any of them.'

They took one look, and decided quite definitely that they couldn't. They had already made up their minds to jump overboard before the thunderous voice of Matron lent speed to their actions.

'All hands abandon ship,' she called out imperiously. 'The magazine's going up any moment.'

It wasn't more than five feet to the ground, and Tony and Mike wasted no time. All the same, they were still in the air when the magazine did go up, and Mike felt something whistle past his ear as he touched the ground. It was extraordinary how quickly the stockpile began to blow up, and for how long it continued to do so.

'You'd better start praying now, Father,' said Matron to the vicar, who was standing nearby. 'That's what we invited you up here for.'

The playground was a blaze of light, and it was hardly necessary for Hugh to put down his switch. However he did so, and then felt it to be his duty to go to the aid of O.W. in the library. His journey was hardly necessary, because the headmaster had flung everything burning into the grate, it was to Hugh's lasting regret that he ever did leave the playground, for he missed all the fun outside.

It will be remembered that Ken had laid out the hose in the expectation of incendiaries landing in the science lab, and his first thought was to retrieve it with the greatest possible speed.

'Come on, fire party,' he shouted, and the fire party was only too anxious to obey the summons. This was the real thing, and very much more exciting than a practice exercise, when the only object which ever got watered was the first eleven cricket pitch. Golightly and the learned Duffield sprinted to the hydrant, whilst Smythe and Macpherson followed the trail of the extended hose. Ken realised that the nozzle should be brought back towards the seat of the flames before the water was turned on, and he and his henchmen grasped the end of the hose. They advanced upon the crowd, who courteously gave way before them, and they would undoubtedly have made an engineering job of the whole business if Flip Flap had not decided to help.

'What on earth is the use of a hose without water?' she asked herself. She scuttled towards the boys at the hydrant, giving them the order 'Water on' in authoritative tones. This was the correct executive word of command, so Duffield had no hesitation in obeying it. For all he knew, the original command had been Ken's, and Flip Flap was merely passing on the good news.

He turned the tap smartly, and the flaccid hose became a writhing serpent. The pressure was excellent, with the result that the party at the other end of the line was taken completely unawares. Caught up and entwined in the coils of the hose, they resembled to a remarkable degree the well-known statue of that unfortunate Trojan gentleman, Laocoon by name, and his sons meeting a tragic end wrapped up in the folds of two gigantic snakes. There was a good photograph of it in Duffield's Latin book, and he did not miss the similarity.

'I say, Golly,' he said, 'Laocoon *ardens* in trouble (*horresco referens*). This is going to be good.'

'What are you talking about, Duffer?' said Golightly, whose foraging into the classical past had nowhere near reached the Second Book of Virgil's *Aeneid*.

'Laocoon was a bloke. He didn't trust the Greeks. *Timeo Danaos et dona ferentis*.'

'Stop spouting Latin at me, Duffer. What's all that got to do with it?' asked the mystified Golightly.

'He was attacked by serpents,' answered Duffield, but he got no further.

The stream of water issuing from the mouth of the snake, which had already reached almost everywhere except the fire itself, scored a direct hit on Duffield, thereby banishing all thought of fiery Laocoon. His entire attention was taken up with turning off the tap, for it was borne in on him that this might now be an excellent idea. Laocoon and his sons regained the initiative, the crowd continued to withdraw to a more respectful distance and Duffield was once more given the operative words.

The fireworks had by this time done all that they were ever going to do, but much of the balcony was made of timber, and it was burning quite nicely. The fire party got to work, and soon doused the flames. It was unfortunate that O.W., having completed his work indoors, should have chosen this moment to see what was cooking outside. He opened the door, was nearly cut in two by the jet of water and stepped onto the balcony. His roar of disapproval was cut short, there was a splintering crash and both balcony and headmaster descended earthwards, the fire having destroyed some vital prop.

'Water off,' called Ken.

There was a dash towards their fallen chief, but there was no question of his not being alive. The well-known Willerby voice, breathing threatenings and slaughter, issued from the ruins. For one who made a point of not swearing in front of the boys, his vocabulary was severely restricted, but he did not noticeably repeat himself whilst he was being picked up, wrung out and felt for broken bones.

The small section of the populace still dry went off at once to the bonfire, whilst the rest of them did some quick-changing. Within a quarter of an hour, O.W. was distributing jumping crackers, producing bangers and generally behaving as he always had behaved. He killed nobody, and the only casualty was a minor burn where a cracker had made its final jump into Golightly's wellington boot. He received adequate medical attention, but it is to be feared that Matron was more concerned with the hole in his stocking than the blister on his calf.

'Ken can't come with me to St Oswald's this afternoon, will you?' asked Hugh. 'I like to have someone with me when the second fifteen's on show.'

It was a couple of days after the firework display, and both the first and second fifteens were playing away there.

'The second fifteen has to contend with an odd pitch, I suppose,' countered Mike.

'Oh, it's all quite civilised. There's no tree within reach.'

'OK then, I'll oblige. The change of scenery will be good fun. What sort of a place is St Oswald's?'

'All right, but they're a bit bowel-conscious. You ought to hear Matron on their system.'

'Bowel-conscious? What do you mean?'

'The boys don't "leave the room" or "be excused". They "take the number".'

'And what exactly is the signification of that?'

'Well, there's a socking great score board, on which there's one set of numbers and a double row of hooks. Each boy has his own number, which he takes into the bogs with him. If the action is successful, he replaces his number on the bottom hook.'

'And an abortive attempt means that it goes back on the top one?'

'Exactly, my dear Watson. All those boys whose numbers are still on the top row by the end of the day get a nice opening medicine.'

'It all sounds indecently revealing, but hardly foolproof. Don't they ever cheat at St Oswald's?'

'I wouldn't be knowing that.'

'Besides, if their boys are anything like ours, they'd forget to shift their numbers.'

'Oh, but health is very much pushed down their throats, like the thermometers which are brought into the form rooms by their matron twice a day.'

'I don't believe that one.'

'It's perfectly true. They solemnly have their temperatures taken every morning and every evening all through the term.'

'Poor little baskets. That's enough to make them feel ill.'

'I know, but you'd think a good many prep schools fussy. Your grammar school was all day boys, but in a full boarding school the entry of any infectious disease is treated rather like leprosy.'

Matron joined them at this point.

'Not in this ship,' she said. 'When I first came to Wintergreen, we were like that. Up went the yellow jack if chickenpox was mentioned.'

'Well, it does play havoc with the teams. I can't stand an epidemic.'

'My dear man, measles is part of a boy's education. If he hasn't had them by the time he's eight, his parents have neglected him, and I take action.'

'What do you do?' asked Mike.

'Expose him to any infection I can lay my hands on. If he's still not had them when he's thirteen, I haven't done an engineering job either.'

'And what diseases have you on the curriculum, Matron?'

'The compulsory list is chickenpox, measles, German measles, whooping cough and mumps – especially mumps.'

'Why?' asked Mike rather injudiciously.

'Have you ever had mumps?' countered Matron.

110

'Yes, I have. I must have been about ten at the time.'

'You were lucky. Another two years, and your testicles might have blown up like barrage balloons.'

Mike looked suitably horrified.

'Do you remember Blenkinsop?' continued Matron, turning to Hugh. 'His were resting on a cushion like the crown jewels for the best part of a week.'

'Yes, I do,' answered Hugh. 'Those blinking mumps lasted for the whole of one summer term, only about two cases at a time. The only school which would play us was Bewd Hall.'

'It's unfortunate, but mumps is the disease with which I have the least success. Some of those juniors simply won't catch it.'

Matron said this with a certain amount of bitterness. She did not like to have to admit even partial defeat. Mike could picture her ordering the microbes to man the uninfected juniors, and putting them on defaulters when they didn't.

'Dilkes has a bit of a sniffle,' Matron continued, 'but I reckon he's fit enough to play.'

'I hope to God he doesn't sneeze in the scrum then,' said Hugh. 'Their referee will be instructed by Mr Arnold to avoid set scrums after the first sneeze, and award a penalty against us each subsequent one.'

'On what grounds?' asked Mike.

'That we are resorting to germ warfare probably,' said Matron.

'From what I've seen of Mr Arnold, all this fussiness doesn't fit in with his character.'

'The man is completely cowed by his matron,' said Hugh unthinkingly. The look on Matron's face was so eloquent that he was forced to add quickly:

'A good idea, mind you, if the matron has any sense.'

'Quite true, Hugh, but that woman's an ass.'

'Arnold's all right,' continued Hugh, 'but he's nothing like as businesslike as he thinks.'

111

'He certainly mucked up his fixture with Bewd Hall. Let's hope he's expecting us today.'

After lunch, a large coach arrived at the door. Both teams piled in, and Matron wished them a fruitful voyage.

'Now then, both teams,' she said, 'mind you win, or you'll get no supper.'

As they moved off, O.W. decided that he might just as well give St Oswald's a ring. He was coming on later in his own car, and he particularly wanted Mr Arnold to lend him some documents, documents which might take some finding. It seemed to him that previous warning could well be a good thing. What he heard on the phone caused him to do some furious thinking, drop everything and follow the bus in swift pursuit.

The journey to St Oswald's takes a good three-quarters of an hour, and it would be against the law of averages if two prep school rugger teams did not contain at least one bad traveller. Psychology, and pills, and a judicious pruning of doubtful starters from teams in away matches can generally avert final catastrophe, but not always. On this particular occasion, Dilkes, who happened to have leanings towards carsickness as well as an incipient cold, was ready to take the appropriate pill at the appropriate moment. He had placed it in his mouth, and was about to swallow it without the aid of water, an achievement of which he was inordinately proud. Unfortunately, it was the only available pill. Even more unfortunately, he sneezed just as he was about to swallow it. He sneezed with zeal and, it is to be feared, without putting his handkerchief to his nose. The pill was projected an unprecedented distance into the unknown – where it stayed. Dilkes was therefore defenceless against the nausea which assailed him at approximately the point of no return on their journey. An urgent entreaty to the driver caused him to take a turning to the left, a lane which incidentally rejoined the main road in about a mile. It was one of those short cuts well known to local experts. If they were hopelessly enmeshed behind a stream of slower-moving traffic, they were tempted to take this route. By going like the clappers, they eventually just failed to get in ahead of the main road queue at the other end. It was a haven of rest for those in urgent need of seclusion, ample parking space and good cover being available.

As the bus pulled up, and poor Dilkes shot out of the door like the cork out of a champagne bottle, a whole fleet of cars going in the opposite direction drew up also, and a small boy left the leading car with equal speed – and with the same urgent mission. He was wearing a brown cap, as were his many companions in the cars. On it was a white cross upon a mound.

Now those familiar with the works of the Venerable Bede, and indeed some of those without even a nodding acquaintance, will know that the saintly King Oswald, before he made an engineering job at Heavenfield, set up a cross upon the field of battle. This cross by all accounts had miraculous powers, and until souvenir hunters did away with it, many remarkable cures were carried out with its aid. The founder of St Oswald's knew his Venerable Bede, so he had no hesitation in choosing a cross for the badge of his school – and this was his school in the cars, or rather the first and second fifteen of that establishment.

'Dr Livingstone, I presume,' said Hugh, as he advanced to meet Mr Arnold.

'What are you doing here?' asked that worthy gentleman.

'We're just coming to play you. Nice of you to meet us.'

'I have an excellent memory,' said Mr Arnold, 'and we fixed up to play at Wintergreen.'

'I think not. The question is, what are we going to do about it?'

'Yes indeed,' said Mr Arnold, thinking of the trouble in store for him if he had to supply the tea.

'I seem to have heard all this before,' murmured Mike. 'Was it a dream, I wonder?'

'Oh dear, oh dear,' sighed Mr Arnold. One extra fifteen might be all right, but two was an impossibility. His school had not the resilience of Wintergreen, and the domestic staff would be shaken, if not utterly defeated. However, a second descent on Wintergreen would hardly be popular.

'We'd better toss for it,' suggested Hugh at last. 'Heads we go on, and tails we turn back. We'll have to stop and do some diplomatic telephoning, though, before we dare show our faces anywhere.'

Whether he won the toss or lost it, Mr Arnold felt that he would be properly in the doghouse with someone. For him there was no reprieve, and this seemed as good a way of settling his fate as any. The coin was still in the air, whilst the opposing leaders stood in the road and watched it, when salvation appeared on the scene with a screech of brakes. Having failed to run both of them over by a hair's breadth, O.W. got out of his car.

'How very fortunate that you're all here,' he shouted. 'It's all fixed up.'

'How nice to see you,' said Mr Arnold. 'What is?'

'What is what?'

'What is fixed up?'

'The rugger, of course. Or are you all out here just for the joy ride?'

'Rather not,' said Mr Arnold, 'but what can we do?'

'The first fifteen's playing at Wintergreen, and the second's at St Oswald's. Tea's being arranged. Do you hear that, boys? All change.'

From seven cars poured out the St Oswald's first team; from the bus were ejected their opponents. For five minutes, there was pandemonium, whilst boots and their owners

114

parted company and were reunited. That two of the St Oswald's car drivers should be parents of second fifteen boys complicated matters considerably, for they were naturally reluctant to ferry the swans, whilst their ugly ducklings turned away from them. Fortunately, O.W.'s car coped with one load, and the other was compressed into the remainder of the fleet.

'Now then, are you all ready?' asked O.W. at last.

A chorus of 'yes, sirs' proclaimed that they were. The drivers of the cars crouched over their respective wheels, and the scene resembled a checkpoint at the Monte Carlo Rally. Mike was in the group of officials on the starting line.

'Tell me, sir,' he said to O.W. 'Why did you choose this lane?'

'Instinct, my boy. Napoleon had it, you know, and called it his star; Joan of Arc referred to it as her voices.'

'And suppose we hadn't been here?'

'Catered for. I dropped a passenger on the main road, with instructions to proceed along it. She ought to be waiting at the end of the lane. You might pick her up, and take her on with you.'

'Her, did you say?'

'Yes, Mike. Guess who.'

'Matron – or perhaps Miss Fellowes,' said Mike with a sinking feeling. She would not be a real help to him in what might be a trying time.

'Certainly not, I wouldn't trust you with either of them.'

Mike was quite pleased to find Ann waiting for him at the end of the lane.

The match bore little resemblance to rugger, or any other game, but a good time was had by all. For the records, St Oswald's amassed twenty-seven points without reply in the first half, possibly whilst Wintergreen got used to the faster turf. In the second half, Wintergreen came into their own, and they scored twenty-five, so, like the Battle of Waterloo, it was a desperately close-run thing. Golightly scored a try, due to some clever thinking by Duffield, much to the surprise and gratification of both of them.

The tea was a triumph, certainly because O.W. had ordered it so authoritatively over the phone. Ann and Mike enjoyed both the game and the feed, but what really made their day was the sight of Golightly keeping watch, and Duffield doing permutations and combinations with the numbers on a gigantic board. There were going to be a good many aperients going down the wrong St Oswald's throats that night, and neither of them saw fit to warn the authorities. Apart from the purely negative action of turning a blind eye on the perpetrators of the atrocity, they did nothing whatever about it.

8

Colonel Dalton's basset hounds were very French, hence the Gallic flavour of their names. They were long-eared, short-legged, flat-footed and incredibly slow, but their noses, *mon dieu,* they were superb. They could follow the scent of a day-old packet of sandwiches, they frequently did, and nothing even remotely edible missed them as they roamed the countryside. Their voices, too, were beautiful to hear. Their ancestors who crossed the Channel had brought a certain garrulity with them, and no pack of foxhounds in the land could rival their music, as they ambled gaily after both existent and non-existent hares.

The Colonel himself was no student of French, and the naming of the puppies with which the pack was frequently blessed was a bit of a problem to him. Sometimes, when a litter had just arrived, he was to be seen examining meditatively the goods which he sold. This close scrutiny of the stock was aimed neither to impress his staff nor to assist him in his duties as managing director of Dalton and Nephew, the wholesale chemists of Elmet. It was merely that he sought inspiration amongst the bottles and cartons and packages for suitable hound names. They must be two-syllabled, French-sounding and distinctly different, the one from the other. Bellair and Bailly, Roussel and Bourjois, Vichy and Celtex had all been found upon the shelves of his warehouse.

It was not, of course, his only source of nomenclature. A good palate accounted for Barsac and Médoc, Bouquet and Sauternes, whilst his general culture was responsible

117

for Gaughin and Renault, Hugo and Ravel. A smattering of sweetly-sounding words, like Centime and Ficelle, Jambon and Voiture, words which he remembered from his schooldays, or from billets behind the lines in World War One, were produced by him with pride, and were pronounced by both himself and Charlie Wise in accents which they themselves considered elegant Parisien. They were sufficiently different from normal hound names to convince the average follower that here was some unique continental flavour to a sport so traditionally English.

Old Willerby had been at school with Colonel Dalton, though the Colonel belonged to an older generation. He was, by all accounts, well over seventy, and rumour had it that O.W. had been his fag. They were firm friends, and the annual meet at Wintergreen was a date to which they both looked forward.

'A grand fellow,' O.W. would say of the Colonel, adding by way of a compliment, 'he treats his hounds just like boys.'

'Old Willerby,' the Colonel would say of him, 'one of the very best. Treats his boys just like hounds. We could do with more of his type, far more of them.'

It was therefore with considerable pleasure that the Colonel and his kennel-huntsman selected the hounds on the Saturday morning of the meet.

'Don't put in Gillette or Champagne,' said the Colonel to Charlie.

'You're maybe right. That'll make twelve and a half couple then,' Charlie replied.

Neither bitch was actually in heat, but it was a bit chancy. Both men could still remember that unforgettable occasion when the entire school had been treated to a practical demonstration on the facts of life during a lull in the hunting. Though regarded by all as the highlight of the afternoon, it was the only occasion within living memory when O.W. had censored some of the boys' Sunday letters.

118

He had made it quite clear that he did not wish a repetition of the performance. Rabelais had been the ardent suitor and, whatever the condition of Pucelle before his attentions, she had certainly lost all claim to the name after them. The result of the union, the Colonel remembered, had been Rainette, Rivoli, Racine and Roubaix – and Racine was the present doyen of his peerless pack.

The selection made, the Colonel took his place beside Charlie in the old Rolls. The joyful chorus of the lucky twelve and a half couple died down as the van gathered speed, but the disappointed howls of anguish of those left behind continued to rend the air long after it had departed from view.

Colonel Dalton was a large, sagging, grey-haired old gentleman, with soulful eyes and a drooping moustache. If any artist had been asked to give his impression of an elderly master of basset hounds, the odds would be heavily on his drawing someone very like Colonel Dalton. The master was impeccably dressed – velvet hunting cap, spotless stock, green coat with purple collar, purple waistcoat, dazzling white breeches and plain green stockings. The hunt stockings had once been purple too, but the Colonel had taken exception to the remark of a friend, who had tactlessly hinted that from a distance he looked like a bishop whose apron had fallen down. The uniform stockings were altered forthwith, for the Colonel was not all that fond of bishops.

They drove on for some miles, discussing hunting prospects and the unpredictable nature of scent. Suddenly, a thought struck Charlie Wise.

'What about giving t'hounds their run?'

'Hounds, what do you mean, Charlie?'

'They'll shit on t'lawn if you don't.'

'God bless my soul, so they will. You're quite right, Charlie, I'd forgotten.'

The very first time that hounds had met at Wintergreen,

119

the press had been there in force, and what could be a better photograph than the Colonel taking his stirrup cup upon the sacred turf, surrounded by his hounds? Unfortunately, the pack had used this hallowed spot as a public convenience, and it was very nearly the last time that the they had been invited to Wintergreen. It was only on the strict understanding that the outrage would not occur again that hounds were tolerated, and even so they were to be kept on the gravel. It was therefore prudent that a timely halt should become routine before the Wintergreen meet.

The van was stopped at a suitable spot, and hounds were decanted upon a grassy verge. All those with inclinations to relieve themselves did so, and they were ushered back into the van.

'Oh, my God,' howled young Ambray. 'What's happening? No hunting?'

It was his first season, and he could not be expected to understand this strange custom. The growl which Racine gave him explained nothing, but it succeeded in shutting him up.

The meet was advertised for twelve-thirty, and punctually at twelve-fifteen the van turned in at the gatehouse. The entire school was already assembled on the gravel, each boy clasping a packed meal. Matron had previously warned them that on no account were they to start eating before hunting started. She had also one further piece of advice.

'Hounds like sandwiches,' she said, 'so keep a sharp lookout, and be prepared to repel boarders.'

Had she not given this sound advice, young Fisher would have gone dinnerless, for within ten seconds of disembarkation Ambray had made a determined but unavailing grab. Retribution followed at once, for Charlie's whip had a long thong, and Charlie knew how to use it. The pack gathered around the master, beseeching him to share with them the drink which he was sipping with relish.

'Good morning, master,' said a gentleman who had just driven up, 'sorry I'm a bit late, but Marguerite insisted on using Galliéni.'

This was Dick Holgate, the first and only whipper-in. He was a slender, middle-aged man, wearing white shorts instead of breeches. He had just climbed out of a small and very ancient Citroen, whose age rivalled that of the Dalton Rolls. He had no hesitation in stationing himself between the pack and the lawn – he knew the drill all right. Mrs Holgate advanced towards the Colonel, cleaving a way through the pack. Since the war, she had lived in England, but she had never lost her delightful French accent. She was very pretty and there were stories going around that she was a princess.

'Good morning, *mon* colonel,' she said. 'Hounds are looking very fit.'

She spoke with the speed of Flip Flap herself, and she had never really mastered the 'th' sound. She also employed what her husband, who taught French at Elmet, was wont to call the uvular 'r'.

'Morning, Marguerite. They *are* fit – I hope Dick's in form. Without him, we'd be sunk.'

'He will go on running,' answered Mrs Holgate. 'He is too old, and one of these days he will drop down dead.'

'Nonsense, my dear. He's as tough as old boots. Have a glass of Willerby's port, it's damned good.'

More cars arrived, and a contingent from the village showed a marked interest in the liquid refreshment. Jack Wright was there, of course, chatting with his usual *bonhomie*. He seemed to know the Holgates quite well, and Mike and Ann, who were standing near Matron, remarked on this.

'Why yes, he met them during the war, and so did I. It was on Marquemique, you know – Father Mirfield married them. Come and be introduced.'

The whipper-in was on his own, still guarding the lawn from intruders, when Matron hailed him.

'Ahoy there, Dick. Come here at once.'

'Oh, hello, Horatia. How are you? I'm on watch – you come to me.'

He didn't seem to be at all afraid of Matron, Mike noted – quite a refreshing change in its way. They went over to him, and Matron made the introductions. His wife joined them, and Ann congratulated them on their car.

'You like old scrap, do you? My wife brought it over with her as her dowry. I have to push most of the time – that's why I wear shorts.'

'It is not true, *chéri*. Your breeches they are too difficult to wash.'

'That's not quite true either, though it's a contributory factor. Actually, my knees are too rheumaticky to stand breeches. Freedom of movement is essential if they're not to seize up altogether.'

'I've been told that you teach at Elmet, sir,' said Mike. 'I've heard quite a bit about the school.'

'Then you have heard about our new headmaster,' said Mrs Holgate brightly. 'He's a proper bastard.'

This was something about which Mike had not heard. Before she could enlarge on his ancestry, however, which she was eager to do in spite of her husband's protests, there was a blast from Charlie's horn, and the pack moved off. Their way lay down the road towards the pub, then by a lane on the right which would take them eventually into the park. Matron had appointed herself field master, and forced the followers to give the hounds plenty of room. She was clad in serviceable tweeds, and her strong right arm wielded a formidable thumb stick.

'I use it when I go otter hunting,' she roared, as a small boy attempted to dodge underneath it, 'but it will do equally well for battering small boys, Balfour.'

Balfour was forced to agree with her.

The Colonel had not gone on with his hounds; he had

retired to the van for his equipment. Not being as mobile as he used to be, he was wont to set up his standard at some point of vantage. In order to keep in touch with the advance guard, he carried a telescope. For his comfort, he wielded an elaborate shooting stick and a kind of waterproof cape which, when unfurled, resembled a bell tent. He also carried a largish flask of excellent brandy, with which he fortified himself at frequent intervals, a fistful of couples and leashes, a map case and a red flag on a pole, the sort of thing which is to be seen on the greens at golf clubs. Had his paraphernalia included a horse, one would have thought that the White Knight had stepped straight through the Looking Glass into rural Yorkshire. Having festooned himself with all his gear, he followed in the wake of the field.

'Come up, my dear fellow, and watch from the gatehouse tower with me,' said O.W. 'You'll get a grand view of the park.'

'No thanks, old boy. I'm for that clump of trees on the skyline. Splendid view all round from there.'

'As you please, old chap. This is liberty hall, you know.'

O.W. stumped up the gatehouse stairs, and the Colonel continued through the gateway and down the road. Field and hounds had passed out of sight round the corner, so he had temporarily lost touch. This did not worry him in the least, for he had told Charlie to draw the park thoroughly before trying the fields beyond it. He didn't think they'd find so soon, but, when almost at the corner, he was astonished suddenly to hear his pack in full cry. There were excited shouts from the boys, desperate blowings of Charlie's horn and a curious series of high-pitched squeals, whose origin baffled the Colonel.

'Might be a cat,' he said to himself. 'Hope they get the beggar – serve it right for upsetting them.'

Actually, it was a very small pig, and nobody saw it join

the party. One moment the pack was composed entirely of basset hounds, and the next a piglet had attached itself to them uninvited.

'Don't look now,' called out Matron to Dick Holgate, 'but you've got a pig in the middle.'

'So we have, this is interesting. Is it yours?'

Hounds were quite unmoved. Noses to the ground and eyes glancing neither to the right nor to the left, they were intent on investigating the fascinating smells on the road. Old Voltaire was puzzled – there was an aroma which smelt delicious, and which he could not for the life of him place. He paused to examine an empty packet of cigarettes.

'Pah! Cork-tipped,' he snuffled to himself. 'Can't possibly be that.'

There was the odd chance that, if the piglet had not lost its nerve, it might have disappeared as silently and as mysteriously as it had come. Had it sidled gently away from hounds, it could possibly have retired up some alleyway unnoticed. Unfortunately, the intruder drew attention to itself. It was an absent-minded little piglet, thinking its own private thoughts. For some yards, it held its course with no idea of the company it was keeping. Suddenly it looked round, saw that it was sailing in the midst of an enemy fleet and panicked. With a wild and piercing squeal, it leapt into the air, landing on Voltaire's broad back. That warrior was startled, it cannot be denied, but the piglet had the greatest difficulty in avoiding his snapping jaws. He did so by retreating aft, falling overboard astern and continuing in headlong and noisy flight. Other jaws snapped close to him, but he cleared the last of the hounds with no more than an inch to spare.

The pack took a second or so to size up the situation and turn, by which time their noble quarry had gained five precious yards and was heading past the whipper-in towards Matron at the rate of knots.

'Let the pig through,' bawled the field master, as she prepared to discourage hounds from following. She failed, however, to whip them off, and they continued in hot pursuit straight into the middle of the boys.

Mike and Ann were in the rear, so they could see nothing of all this. Suddenly, there was indescribable chaos ahead, then a piglet appeared out of the scrum. It gained a good ten yards on the pack, which undoubtedly saved its life, for twelve and a half couple of basset hounds then broke through in full cry. Never in their lives had they hunted so well together – the traditional blanket covered the lot. They had proceeded fifteen yards or more before the boys could disentangle themselves, and then they also took up the chase.

'Oh Mike,' said Ann, 'isn't this wonderful? They're all going straight back to school.'

The piglet met the Colonel at the corner, shooting between his legs. The pack had gained appreciably, and they were so close on its heels that the Colonel could do nothing to stop them. He drew his silver hunting horn from between the top buttons of his coat, and prepared, like Roland with his oliphant, to blow himself inside out in an effort to retrieve the day. Again like Roland, he was far too late. The hounds were upon him, and around him and on top of him before he had coaxed one dulcet note from his horn.

Had he been able to call them, it is conceivable that his hounds might have obeyed the summons. Charlie's horn, like the majority of hunting horns, sounded the note 'D', but the Colonel's sounded 'A'. The pack knew this; they also knew that, when the Colonel used his horn, instant obedience was expected of them. Its message was invariably an urgent one, and they had been trained to drop everything and rally on him. Already that season its clarion call had given them the following messages:

125

(a) The cows which you are rounding up are accompanied by a bull. Rally on me.
(b) The owner of the hens amongst whom you are disgracing yourselves is approaching with a shotgun. Rally on me.
(c) The hare which you are pursuing with such zeal along the railway line is about to meet head-on the 3.14 down train. Rally on me.

What is more, every single time that a meal was ready, the Colonel sounded his horn, and the message which he gave the pack was – 'Dinner is served. Rally on me.' So far, they always had obeyed the summons, but this would have been the severest test of all. The question of their obedience, however, is purely academic for, as has been mentioned already, the horn of the hunter was silent.

Old Willerby was watching from his gatehouse tower. Into the straight came the piglet, and the hounds, and the boys, and the hunt servants, and then the adult members of the field. All of them were giving tongue, but the music of the pack was loudest. O.W. had just the time to note that his matron was attending to the fallen master before a thought so awful struck him that all else paled into insignificance.

Unless he did something about it, and darned quickly, the whole lot of them would be through the gateway and surging over his precious lawn. This would never do, and the means of salvation was at his disposal. Feverishly, he unlashed the helm – and down crashed a portcullis. He had no clear intention either of saving the piglet or of delivering it swiftly into the jaws of the expectant pack. They had gained, and no more than one foot separated the agitated spiral of the piglet's tail from the gnashing jaws of the leading hounds. A row of spikes flashed down in front of the piglet, but he shot through the square hole which providentially appeared before his perspiring face.

The pack pulled up as if with a scream of brakes. Not one of their number was able even to start squeezing through. Frustrated and foiled of their prey, they demonstrated their disappointment in no uncertain way.

And then, quite clearly, the note of 'A' from a silver horn sounded at their rear. With commendable speed, they returned to their lord and master, who was fortunately none the worse for his spill.

It might be thought that anything else that happened that hunting day would be in the nature of an anticlimax, but this was not the case. The appetites of hounds, hunt servants and field were merely whetted. As they retraced their steps towards the park, Dick Holgate, who always wrote the accounts for *Horse and Hound,* called out to the Colonel.

'Shall I say it was a sharp two minutes after the pig?'

'Make it five,' answered the Colonel, 'and don't forget the portcullis – it's unusual.'

'I'd call a piglet unusual enough, master. We've nearly had a squirrel, a brace of tawny owls and old Lady Canton's peacocks in our time, but pork's unique in our annals.'

'There's always a first time, you know. Now I come to think of it, we'll prolong the chase to seven minutes; sounds better.'

Each week, *Horse and Hound* contains reports of goodish runs, and it is to be hoped that such immoral tactics are not normally employed in their compilation.

Once through the gate into the park, Charlie encouraged the pack with largely unintelligible noises. Young Lisette had to be severely reprimanded for an unsuccessful attack on a small bird, thought by the naturalists in the party to be a fieldfare.

''ware wing, Lisette,' said Dick, cracking his whip ferociously.

127

'What, me?' howled Lisette. Her look implied that this was a gross miscarriage of justice, and that she had shown marked forbearance when the fieldfare twittered ruderies at her.

Meanwhile, the Colonel had selected a caddy from a score of youthful volunteers. Golightly knew when he was on to a good thing, and was gratified that he should be the chosen one. At the cost of a little light porterage, he had established himself on the headquarters' staff. He would see all the fun without having to move far from base, so he trod happily in his master's steps towards the clump of trees, bearing all the accoutrements except the brandy. The Colonel himself clutched that; the young must not be corrupted, and anyway, a clumsy squire might shatter the most valuable part of his armament.

Barely had they reached their point of vantage, when Dauphine gave tongue. It was only the faintest whimper, but the old bitch did not lie and several of the others joined her. They were in no doubt about it, and for forty yards they followed the line vociferously. Matron restrained the field, which showed a tendency to shoot ahead of her, and her fiercest look caused an unnatural silence.

'Give hounds a chance, lads,' she said, quite quietly for her. 'They haven't found yet.'

There was a check, and eager snuffling noses quartered the ground. Purposefully, Racine ambled onwards, his stern feathering. This, he thought, was a hare, indubitably a hare. Somewhere close at hand he would find a hare. Suddenly, the scent came stronger; he savoured it, and recognised it.

'It's not just any old hare,' he sang. 'Come here, lads and lasses. It's a Wintergreen hare – and it's not just any old Wintergreen hare. It's THE hare, the one we nearly had last year; we'll get the bastard this time.'

Old Racine was perhaps a trifle coarse, but when one is old and very excited, one's language tends to deteriorate in the heat of the moment. It was THE Wintergreen hare, he knew, and his friends must share the joy of it with him. Overcome with emotion, he sat down to give tongue the better, and twelve couple of his fellows rallied to the call.

The Wintergreen hare was an old campaigner. He knew that his ancient foes, the basset hounds, were all around him, but he wasn't going to move unless he had to. If the worst came to the worst, and in his experience it didn't half the time, he would leap up in their midst, scare the living daylights out of them, swerve his way through the whole blooming pack of them and lead them the very Dickens of a chase.

But he wasn't reckoning on Racine sitting on top of him.

For the fraction of a second, Racine's broad posterior settled on something soft and warm, something which gave an outraged, almost human scream and wriggled. It was a terrible shock to both old gentlemen. Racine's deep, manly voice rose an octave or two, turning into a frightened puppy-like howl as he shot vertically into the air. He hadn't moved so quickly for years but, fast as he rocketed upwards, he was overtaken in mid-flight by the Wintergreen hare. It was instinct which caused Racine's jaws to snap, and they closed upon the fur on the back of his unfortunate quarry.

'He's got me, by jabers,' was the hare's first thought.

'I've got him, by jabers,' was Racine's.

It was with considerable relief that the hare felt a mouthful of fur come out. After all, a sore back was better than total annihilation.

'Damn and blast,' said Racine, as he spat out the fur. 'Come and help me chaps. Didn't you see? I nearly had him.'

'The hare shot off at considerably greater speed than was his wont. Generally, 'half ahead' was sufficient to outdistance the pack, but he was very considerably put out. Charlie gave some remarkably bloodcurdling calls, and both hounds and field surged forward with a gay abandon.

'He's turning to starboard,' said Matron knowingly after a few moments, and she attracted a fair following of the less fleet of foot. Most scientifically, she calculated the diameter of the hare's circle.

The hare veered to port.

Nine times out of ten a hare runs in a wide circle, so wide that it is often difficult to tell whether it is running left-handed or right-handed for the first few hundred yards. Matron's inspired guesswork, had it been right, would have raised her prestige enormously. Being wrong, it turned the hunting into a nice country walk for herself and her protégés. It was quite three-quarters of an hour before her party rejoined the main body.

Having clapped his telescope to his eye and followed the hare's progress for some considerable time, the Colonel sent Golightly fourth with the red flag. By means of sundry signals, he directed him to the exact locality of the hare's seat, and ordered him to stick the pole into the ground. Sooner or later, the hare would come back to this spot, and the Colonel liked to watch it. The placing of the marker was of very great assistance to him, but it must not be thought that he was taking an unfair advantage of the quarry. Even if he saw the hunted hare return to its form, he considered it unsporting to lift hounds. They had to find the spot for themselves, and, though they did occasionally do this, many a hunt finished with the pack searching diligently in quite the wrong field – and the hare laughing at them uproariously from beneath the shadow of the Colonel's flag.

Golightly had hardly returned to his post, when the hare came lolloping into sight. His first fast burst had taken him far ahead of the baying pack, but scent was good and he could hear that they were still in very fine voice. He decided that a little rest could do no possible harm. To tell the truth, the narrowness of his escape and the speed with which he had covered the first half mile had blown him considerably. With a bit of luck, he thought, they'd change onto the line of a bumptious cousin of his. He'd gone into his territory, and passed within a couple of leaps of his seat. Do the fellow good to be chased around for a bit. He cocked his ears to listen for a tell-tale change in the tempo of the music of the hounds, a change which would inform him that cousin Bertie had taken to his heels, and was being followed by the pack. Time passed, and there was no such change – the pack was getting appreciably nearer each minute. At last, the Wintergreen hare decided that the time had come to make a move. He gave an almighty leap from his resting place, doubled up one furrow and down the next, jumped sideways to confuse the issue even further and continued leisurely on his 'great circle' course.

'Look at that, my boy,' said the Colonel. 'You wouldn't have seen that if you'd been charging madly after hounds, would you?'

'No, sir,' answered Golightly. In Matapan that night, his companions would be hearing of the supernatural cunning of the hare.

Five minutes later, hounds arrived, followed by Dick Holgate and Mike. They watched the pack charge up the furrow, and then hurtle back the way they had come.

'What is happening?' asked Mike.

'Hare's doubled. Didn't they work out the line beautifully? These boys are slow, but they know the tricks.'

The pack was off again before anyone else appeared on the scene. The hare had selected a route which entailed the crossing of Dog Dyke, a meandering watercourse, no fewer than four times. There is nothing quite like a wide ditch, preferably carrying plenty of water, to spreadeagle the field. Dick plunged boldly through each time, and Mike had been able to leap the ditch, but others, including Charlie, spent a good deal of time hesitating on the brink.

Charlie eventually decided that a crossing was not necessary, and collected up the waverers.

Anderson and Stevenson, however, had no intention of abandoning the exercise. Being gentlemen of resource, they would certainly have completed all four crossings in good order, but they were determined not to get their feet wet and possessed but one navigable left foot seaboot between them. Each crossing entailed this watertight wellington being used by one of them for wading, and then hurled back across the dyke in exchange for the leaker. In this way, both boys remained dry-shod, but the manoeuvre naturally took up time. They did well enough until the final crossing, when Stevenson's unerring aim faltered. He had just crossed over, and was casting back the good boot, when his foot slipped. Even a first fifteen scrum half does occasionally send out a poor pass, especially when he is standing on one leg. Anyway, Anderson was quite unable to take it, and the boot finished up in mid-stream. It floated gently eastwards with the current, half full of water and slowly turning.

'Now you've done it, Steve. That's my boot,' said Anderson.

'Chuck mine across then, Andy, and I'll fish it out.'

'I will not, you fool. I'll do the fishing.'

Anderson realised that his friend's unseaworthy boot was considerably better than none at all, and he was dashed if he was going to part with it. He made several abortive attempts to collect up his property until, goaded by Stevenson's rude remarks, he gave up.

'Very well, then,' he shouted. 'You see if you can do any better.'

In a fit of passion, he took off the boot, and hurled it in the general direction of Stevenson. There were then two left boots floating upon the surface of the waters. This led to even more furious altercation as they followed the wellingtons on their long journey to the sea. It was fortunate that the current was weak, since both boys were able to keep in touch by means of a series of elegant hops. They were becoming more and more irate, and there would undoubtedly have been bloodshed had they not been separated by the dyke. They were making such a frightful row that it was no small wonder that they attracted attention. Matron and her party hove into sight.

'What on earth are you two up to?' she thundered.

'Hi, Matron, come here, please,' said Anderson. 'That fool Stevenson has thrown my boot in the dyke.'

'And what about you, Anderson? What do you think you've done with mine?'

'He threw mine in first, Matron. It was a rotten shot.'

'And so was his. Please, Matron, may we borrow your stick please?'

'Certainly not. I don't want that in the drink too.'

At this stage, they came upon a rather insecure plank bridge, and the boots were retrieved in triumph. The argument still went on but, before the actual onset of battle, Matron threatened to set about the pair of them if they did not shut up. They poured the water disconsolately out of the boots, put them on with the maximum amount of fuss and the whole collection of them trudged onwards, guided now by the sound of the pack. Their luck had turned, and the hunt was swinging towards them.

'Look,' said Matron suddenly. 'Here comes the hunted hare. Crouch down, and don't say a word.'

The whole party tried to sink into the ground and, anyway, the hare was too busy with the pack to see what was in front of him. He had just failed for the fourth time to confound his enemies by running through a flock of sheep, and he had already lost his temper.

'Oh, hell,' he said to himself, as he nearly cannoned into Matron. 'These people will be the death of me.'

He swerved aside, and Anderson picked up a fair-sized clod of earth, flinging it with remarkable accuracy at the retreating hare. He was a better shot with earth than he was with boots. It would be difficult to say whether the hare or Matron was the more scandalised. These ruddy boys were worse than hounds, thought the hare ruefully.

'Anderson, I thought I told you to crouch down and be quiet,' said Matron.

'Please, Matron, I did and I was.'

'But you threw something at the hunted hare. Not a bit sporting – and it could spoil the scent.'

'Sorry, Matron,' said Anderson meekly. He didn't see why it should spoil the scent, and on his farm he always threw the nearest thing that came to hand at any passing hare, but he was all for a quiet life.

Up came the pack, or rather most of it. Dick was at this moment chastising a detachment consisting of Ambray, Tristran, Vichy and Joyeuse, all of whom had decided that it might be a good idea to chase the sheep by way of a change. Mike and Ann were the first followers up; they were just in time to see Matron putting hounds on the line. She knew quite well that the Colonel would not approve, but hoped that his telescope was not at this moment pointing in her direction.

'Nobody up with them, as usual,' she roared. 'You can't expect hounds to hunt on their own all the time.'

The purist might not have agreed with her, but the pack seemed quite grateful for her assistance.

'Come along,' she continued. 'We'll get this hare on our own.'

They proceeded for a quarter of an hour before a check enabled the rest of the field to catch up. Matron handed over to Charlie, well satisfied with her handling of the pack.

'Come on, Charlie,' she said. 'The hare's dead beat, probably clapped in this field.'

And Matron was quite right. He was tired, and he had stopped here for necessary repairs. An hour of this mad

134

chase was a bit too much of a good thing, he thought, and something must be done about it. He wasn't going to risk Racine sitting on him again, so he set off before any of the pack had reached within twenty yards of him. He tried to escape unobtrusively up a furrow, for they were on ploughland, but he was spotted by Lisette.

'Good little bitch that,' said Charlie. He felt that she deserved some praise, even if she did not always confine her interests to hares. She hadn't been in the foray with the sheep anyway.

The rest of the pack followed Lisette in full cry, and the Wintergreen hare decided that he was going to call on his cousin again. But he must gain ground. Whether it was sheer luck or very careful planning, no one will ever know, but he selected a route which led the pack across a large field of the prickliest stubble imaginable. Up to this moment, they were going splendidly, and were losing very little ground.

'Oh, my God, my feet. This is killing me,' grumbled Racine, as he slowed to a walk. The others followed suit. There was nowhere free from the spikes, and the greater part of the pack, whose footprints resembled those of the Hound of the Baskervilles rather than any ordinary canine, suffered agonies.

'I'm not going through this, girls,' wailed Princesse, and she and a few more elderly matrons forsook the hunt altogether, walking back to the edge of the field and trotting round the circumference.

'Just look at those bitches. What's come over them?' asked Matron, turning to Mrs Holgate, her nearest neighbour.

'Don't you understand? It is their tits, they touch the ground,' replied that keen observer. 'If you were in their position, Horatia, you would turn back too.'

It took some considerable time to reunite the pack, and no one was in sight when the Wintergreen hare approached once more his cousin's form.

'Thank God you're in, Bertie,' he panted. 'Be a good chap and take over – I'm about all in.'

'Not on your life, chum,' said Bertie. 'I'm staying here.'

It was fortunate for the Wintergreen hare that hounds did not see him eject young Bertie by force at the crucial moment. All they did see was a hare going flat out ahead of them, and they increased the volume of their joyful song of praise. Old Racine was doubtful; he shook his head in a puzzled sort of way, for there was an indefinable difference about the scent. Then he went on after the others. At his age, he simply could not afford to dawdle, for it was all that he could do to keep up sometimes nowadays. All the same, he hoped to be able to manage just one more season.

It was with a sigh of huge relief that the Wintergreen hare sank down to rest in his cousin's form. He stayed there whilst his cousin did a couple of flashy circles. When all was quiet, he got up stiffly and ambled back to his own home. He proceeded with caution, and it was just as well that he did, or he would have run slap into a stoutish twelve-year-old. This boy was removing a red flag from his doorstep.

'What's that ruddy boy doing with that ruddy flag?' he asked himself, but he was too darned tired to worry over the problem for long.

9

The only person about the school who did not enjoy the visit of the basset hounds was Hugh Williams. It was not that he was in sympathy with the League Against Cruel Sports, he wouldn't have minded people chasing after anything at the right time, but here was a glorious afternoon, an afternoon which ought to have been devoted to rugger, squandered on a pastime so vile that in its pursuit no ball whatsoever was employed. He went down to the rugger field in a sulk, and had a training session all on his own. His adoring wife did stroll down to have a look at him, but he saw nothing of anybody else. Had either hare or hounds invaded his privacy, he would probably have eased his feelings by taking an impartial drop-kick at them. He finished up in a filthy temper, a state of affairs only slightly improved by the sight of the magnificent spread. He had no hesitation in helping the hunters to dispose of it but, towards the end of the meal, his presence was required by the duty prefect on a matter of some urgency.

'What's the matter, Duffield?' he asked rather crossly. 'Can't you see I'm having my tea?'

'I am sorry to disturb you, sir, but I have ascertained that you are the duty master today.'

'Am I? Oh, well, what about it?'

'There has arisen, sir, a somewhat awkward situation. Clark here tells me...'

Duffield had under his wing a rather unpleasant little boy in Mike's form. He was the only child in a family which was almost revoltingly rich. It was always a toss-up whether he would be collected in one of the chauffeur-driven works limousines, in his father's Bentley or in his mother's very flashy sports car with more gears than any automobile has a right to possess. Everything that Clark owned, and he owned a great deal, was of the very best quality – and he did not hesitate to let everyone know about it. Moreover, he was not at all keen on letting his companions do more than admire his property from a distance.

The mention of his name caused Clark to break into the conversation with a vigour which would have been most telling if only Hugh could have understood a word.

'Now then, Clark,' he said, 'take a grip of yourself, and don't behave like a disturbed anthill.'

Clark took a deep breath, and tried again.

'Sir, please sir, someone has stolen my stamps.'

When small boys mislay, even temporarily, their property, their first reaction is generally that a crime has been committed.

'Stolen? You've probably left them lying around,' said Hugh scathingly.

'I assumed that myself, sir,' chipped in Duffield, 'but I have ascertained that the album is not missing. Clark alleges that some valuable stamps have been removed from it without the owner's permission.'

'Well ascertained. Let's have a look at the album.'

'I deemed it more prudent, sir, not to advertise the loss just yet.'

'Oh, why's that, Duffield?'

'Do you think I might confer with you in private, sir?'

'All right, Sherlock Holmes. You buzz off, Clark, the matter is in safe hands.'

'And inform no one else as to what has happened,' added Duffield severely, inferring that complete secrecy would aid the police in their inquiries.

'Now then, Duffield, what's all the mystery?'

'Well, sir, Clark's in the third form.'

'I know he is. What's that got to do with it?'

'So is Knightley, sir.'

'Aha, Duffield, I see your point. Say no more.'

Knightley was the school kleptomaniac. Any preparatory school which does not occasionally have a light-fingered pupil is distinctly lucky, for the investigations which are set in train when anything really does disappear are extremely hard work and frequently unprofitable. Sometimes, the thief is never discovered, which is unfortunate for him in the long run. Poor Knightley, on the other hand, was always discovered, and his parents, who were a most respectable and God-fearing couple, were absolutely horrified. At the first onset of the malady, manifested in a liking for other boys' Dinky cars, they had wept on O.W.'s shoulder, saying that they would seek medical advice.

'If you must, you must,' said O.W., 'but these trick cyclists don't know as much about boys as I do. Leave him to me, and I'll cure him.'

Knightley was caught out seven times his first year and five his second; this looked like being the first theft of his third academic year. It was routine stuff for Hugh, and, the sooner he passed on the buck, the sooner he could finish his tea. Clark was in Mike's form, so was Knightley – so Mike was the bloke to start running round in small circles.

'Thank you, Duffield,' he said. 'You might watch Knightley discreetly and see if you can find out where he hides the stamps. Let Mr Thornton know if you have any luck. Oh, we had to dig up the rockery for Hudson's coin collection; you might bear that in mind.'

The duty master then explained the situation to Mike over the last of some particularly succulent cake. His duty done, he lost interest – neither Clark nor Knightley would ever make the first fifteen, and he washed his hands of such second-class citizens.

Mike could have put the matter straight into O.W.'s hands, but that would have been dull for a young man whose girlfriend was going to be a policewoman. A little private investigation was called for, so he got in touch with the law.

'Now, Ann, let's get the facts established before I tell O.W. Shall we pull in Knightley for questioning?'

'No, let's conduct a search. We don't need a warrant to look through his things.'

Curiously enough, the prefect on duty felt much the same, so Mike and Ann were continually running into Duffield during their researches. After the third encounter, up to which time they had all of them tried to look as if they were doing something entirely different, they decided to pool their resources. They rapidly came to the conclusion either that the swag had already been cached or else that the stamps were secreted upon Knightley's person. Between the three of them, desk, tuck-box, locker and drawers had been searched diligently without result. What is more, neither Knightley nor anyone else knew what the bloodhounds were up to.

It was providential that it should be a Saturday evening, for all Knightley's clothing could be taken away from him at bedtime without his suspecting that it was to be examined with the thoroughness of a forensic laboratory test. Shirts and stockings and underclothes were all clean for Sunday, and the shorts and jersey were swapped for suits. It was routine for the latter to be gathered up and inspected, so Ann's action in collecting every stitch of Knightley's Saturday raiment was quite normal. Duffield was confident that the criminal had had no opportunity whatsoever to get rid of the stolen stamps.

Matron saw Ann with the bundle and, on hearing that it belonged to Knightley, told her assistant that the lot would probably need fumigating.

'He's been looking as if he'd come straight out of the scran bag the last two days,' she said.

'What's a scran bag exactly, Matron?' asked Ann.

'You ought to know that by now, Miss Pinkerton. It's where all the lost property goes.'

'Is it a naval term, Matron?' chipped in Anderson, who happened to be listening, 'like a nest of bastards?'

'Don't interrupt, Anderson.'

'Sorry, Matron, but is it?'

'Yes, Anderson, it is. You can, however, use the term in any society. If dining with royalty, I should advise you to avoid employing your phrase.'

'Yes, Matron,' said Anderson.

A thorough investigation of all pockets and possible hiding places revealed the following – two very dirty handkerchiefs, three short pieces of string, a crumpled and unopened letter from home, a half-used piece of chewing gum, a ring out of a Christmas cracker, a Cub badge, a nappy pin, page seventeen of *Kennedy's Shorter Latin Primer* and a slip of paper on which was the mysterious message – NBUSPO JT B GPPM. There was, however, no sign of valuable stamps from Clark's album.

Foiled of her original objective, Ann turned to the coded message.

'Ordinary substitution code, I should think,' she announced learnedly.

'I don't mind betting it says that somebody's a fool,' said Mike.

'What makes you so sure?'

'Oh, the odds are heavily on a coded sentence containing an announcement of that nature.'

'You are perfectly correct in your assumption, sir,' said Duffield, who had been peering at the message too. 'The writer has gone one letter forward each time. A is B, and B is C.'

'And who is the fool?' asked Ann.

'Matron appears to be the subject of the sentence.'

'She will be pleased if I tell her,' said Mike, 'but this isn't getting our detection any further. I suppose I'd better report the matter to Mr Willerby.'

'It would be prudent, sir,' said Duffield regretfully. He was just beginning to get his teeth into the problem, and had secretly wondered whether to go over the rockery with a trowel, just in case history repeated itself.

'Stamps,' said O.W. scornfully. 'I'd ban the things if I didn't know that the number of collectors would be doubled. A forbidden hobby is so much more interesting.'

'It seems quite a harmless pastime, sir.'

'Harmless? They're more trouble than they're worth. It's nearly impossible to establish ownership of the beastly things, but we've a cast-iron case here – it's Knightley.'

'I'm not so sure.'

'Oh, yes, it's Knightley all right, up to his old tricks again.'

'We have carried out a fairly thorough search, sir.'

'Don't you worry, Mike. I'll get him to tell me all about it in ten minutes. This'll be the thirteenth time – and darned unlucky for him, I may say. It's Attila for him without a doubt.'

'Do you beat him every time he's caught stealing?'

'Oh, no, I ring the changes. He never knows what I'll do next – very subtle, I am. Once I never punished him at all, but he whipped Flip Flap's silver pencil the following week and got a double ration that time.'

'Does he always admit the theft?'

'In the end, yes, but there has to be a token denial at the start. Mind you, he used to admit to thefts which he hadn't committed – and that was awkward.'

'Why on earth did he do that?'

'To oblige, I think, but he's grown out of that one.'

'When will you see him?'

'First thing tomorrow. It will give his conscience time to get working.'

But if Knightley had a guilty conscience, it did not spoil his night's sleep. He seemed genuinely surprised when he was summoned to O.W.'s study after breakfast. For a quarter of an hour, he denied all knowledge of a theft of any kind. He fell into none of the traps which O.W., in his rather elephantine way, had set to ensnare him, and he appeared to be ignorant both of the nature of the booty and of the identity of the victim.

'Please, sir, what's been stolen from who?'

Up to this point, O.W. had carefully refrained from mentioning both Clark and his stamps, but now he was forced to reveal that there were gaps in that gentleman's collection. He had thought it likely that he could have persuaded Knightley to divulge this information, in which case the prisoner would have known too much about the theft to continue protesting his innocence for long.

'But I don't collect stamps, sir,' went on Knightley with an air of such terribly injured innocence that his interrogator had to admit temporary defeat.

'Very well, Knightley,' said O.W., 'this is your last chance. I must warn you that, if you don't own up now, and you are found out later, I shall ask your parents to take you away from here. I am ready to help you if you want help.'

It did cross Knightley's mind that owning up could be a kind of insurance against this terrible eventuality, for he was very fond of Wintergreen, but he hardened his heart.

'I didn't take the stamps, sir, honestly I didn't,' he said.

This was really most annoying, but O.W. very nearly believed him. He called an extraordinary general meeting to thrash out the problem, at which he paraded Attila in front of the entire school. His harangue was so devastating that even the most innocent began to wilt.

'I shall give the boy who has taken those stamps just half

143

an hour to own up,' he roared, and the assembly disintegrated in shocked silence.

'What on earth happens if no one does own up?' asked Mike, as he discussed the edict in the staff common room.

'Your guess is as good as mine,' answered Tony, 'but he has been known to beat the whole school.'

'But that's grossly unfair.'

'Not to O.W. After all, if he thrashes the lot of them, except Clark of course, he would know that the culprit had not escaped him.'

'I'd include Clark too,' said Ken. 'It would do him no harm, and he could have taken the ruddy things just to draw attention to himself.'

Fortunately, the half hour had not yet expired when Hugh Williams arrived on the scene with a look of smug superiority on his face.

'No barbaric mass execution,' he said. 'The problem is now solved. Whilst you have been gassing here, I've been working. Just you guess where I found these.'

'In Clark's desk,' answered Ken, gazing at the missing stamps.

'Clark's? Don't he a twit. They were in Knightley's. I told you he took them.'

Very pleased with himself, he went off to report his find to O.W., and Mike departed in the other direction to confer with his associates. He could not contact Duffield at first, but he got hold of Ann. When she heard the news, she was most put out, for she had already crossed Knightley off her list of suspects. She was almost sure that she had found the real culprit, and now her deductions seemed to have been wildly off the mark. As she was voicing her disappointment, Duffield sidled up, looking conspiratorial.

'I have been employed in tailing Knightley,' he said, adding with evident regret, 'but I observed nothing suspicious before Mr Willerby summoned him once more.'

'Well, Duffield, it's all over. Mr Williams has found the stamps in Knightley's desk. He must have transferred them from some secret hiding place.'

'He can't have done that, sir.'

'But he has, Duffield, he has,' said Mike.

'No, sir. Knightley did not transfer them.'

'Don't be silly. How can you possibly know?'

'Please, sir, I am perfectly certain.'

'I quite agree with you, Duffield, but we can't prove it,' said Ann sympathetically.

'But I am confident that I can, Miss Pinkerton.'

'How?' asked Mike and Ann together.

'Because I inspected his desk again just before the assembly – and I ascertained that they were not there.'

'Well, he must have slipped them in later,' said Mike.

'But I informed you, sir, that I was tailing him,' replied Duffield patiently. 'It is absolutely certain that he went nowhere near his desk.'

'There now,' interrupted Ann, 'that proves his innocence, and I have a good line on someone else.'

'It is absolutely imperative that we should report this matter at once,' went on Duffield.

'Couldn't I have a little more time to complete my inquiries?' asked Ann.

'You carry on. Duffield and I will have to hurry if we are to avert an assault on Knightley's person,' said Mike.

'That is my own feeling exactly,' said Duffield, and he and his assistant charged off to defend the innocent against aggression.

Ann went off in search of her suspect, another third-former, called Cuckfield. It boded ill for him that she should be carrying a little black notebook at the ready, and she was mentally licking her pencil in joyful anticipation.

She ran her suspect to earth in Matron's room. He was pasty-faced and shifty-eyed, and he had just reported sick.

'May I have a word with this boy?' asked Ann icily.

'Why, yes. I don't know what's the matter with him. Temperature's normal and bowels open.'

'It's guilty conscience, Matron.'

'That wouldn't surprise me at all. I suspected something of the sort.'

'Now then, Cuckfield,' said Ann, turning to her suspect, 'I have reason to believe that you can help me with my inquiries.'

'Yes, Miss Pinkerton,' said Cuckfield in a miserable whisper. He was not quite sure what it was all about, but he suspected the worst.

'Speak up, boy,' bellowed Matron. 'Do you collect stamps?' asked Ann.

'Yes, Miss Pinkerton.'

Ann took a short while to write this in her notebook, and Cuckfield suffered acutely. His suspicions were clearly justified.

'Have you looked at Clark's collection recently?'

'No, Miss Pinkerton.'

'That's a lie for a start,' broke in Matron. 'I heard you telling Anderson only the other day that a little squirt like Clark didn't deserve to have such super stamps.'

'Well...' started Cuckfield, but then sought refuge in silence.

'Well, what?' roared Matron.

'Well, yes.'

'There you are,' said Matron in triumph, 'but carry on Miss Pinkerton.'

'Now think very carefully, and tell me when you last saw Clark's album.'

'I don't know, Miss Pinkerton.'

'I think you do. It was yesterday, wasn't it?'

'It might have been.'

There was another long pause whilst Ann wrote, and on

146

could feel the silence biting into her victim. She then continued relentlessly with her questions, questions which concerned Cuckfield's feelings and his actions during the last twenty-four hours. Helped by what might be termed a hostile witness in the background, she soon reduced the already demoralised Cuckfield into a state bordering on complete collapse.

'Now you took those stamps, didn't you?' she asked.

'No, Miss Pinkerton,' came from Cuckfield's lips, but very unconvincingly.

'I think you did. It would be much better for you if you owned up, you know.'

'Far better,' broke in Matron.

'As soon as Mr Willerby spoke to the school, you got frightened, took the stamps from where you had hidden them and planted them in Knightley's desk. It wasn't a very nice thing to do, was it?'

'No, Miss Pinkerton.'

'So you did put them there?'

'Of course he did,' said Matron before he could reply, 'and a very shabby trick too.'

'You deliberately chose Knightley because he had taken things before. Now you did take those stamps, didn't you?'

Cuckfield felt that this purgatory might go on for ever, Ann's lighter salvos being backed up by Matron's fifteen-inch guns. Even just retribution was better than this.

'Yes, Miss Pinkerton,' he said at last.

Ann shut her notebook with a snap.

'That's better,' she said. 'Now we had better go to Mr Willerby and get it over.'

'Yes, Miss Pinkerton,' said Cuckfield tearfully.

'I'm coming too,' said Matron, and she it was who led the convoy into O.W.'s study.

For some time, the situation there had been a little confused. First of all, Mike and Duffield had had the greatest

147

difficulty in persuading O.W. that they were rescuing Knightley, and were not further witnesses for the prosecution. The poor boy himself took a little time to appreciate that the visitors were on his side. He had almost been convinced by events that he had taken the stamps after all, but he came round to the theory of his own innocence rather sooner than did O.W. The latter was most reluctant to believe Mike and Duffield. Apart from anything else, he tended to treat Attila as a Gurkha treats his kukri. Once it had been drawn, it was against his principles to return it to its resting place before blood had been let.

When prisoner and escort joined the party, he needed some persuading that there was a second kleptomaniac in one small class. It didn't seem fair or reasonable to him, and action was delayed, first of all whilst Ann went methodically through the evidence which led to the arrest and then whilst Matron pointed out how thoroughly ungentlemanly, unsporting and unseamanlike this defaulter had been. The words 'sadly lacking in O.L.Q.' thundered forth, with an explanation aside to Ann that the letters meant 'officer-like quality'. Finally, O.W. realised that Attila need not be laid aside unused.

'The six of the best were plainly audible, and those who later paid for a close-up view of the damage noted that, in spite of his age, O.W.'s grouping was still magnificent. The stripes were measured with the aid of Anderson's ruler, and it was agreed that thirty-three millimetres covered the lot

As for Cuckfield, suffice to say that he was discouraged from ever again taking his neighbour's goods. He wasn't really a bad lad, and he had gained greatly from his painful lesson. During the discussion in the staff room afterwards Topsy produced the information that in one of his former schools there had been no fewer than four kleptomaniacs in a class of seven.

Small boys are quite unpredictable at times, for the whole

incident added to Clark's rather than to Cuckfield's unpopularity. Knightley was so relieved to find that he had not stolen anything after all, that he was almost grateful to the individual who had put him so thoroughly on the spot. Clark had never been exactly appreciated, and this incident did not help him in the least. It must be admitted that quite often he had rather a poor time of it; he whined so delightfully when provoked, and it was safe to assume that he was incapable of hitting back. His companions were not vicious bullies, though these do exist in every school from time to time. They showed, however, a nastiness of nature which did them no credit. Anderson and Stevenson especially led him a rare old dance during the next week or so. The staff were not blind to this, and words were said about it, but the baiting went cheerfully on.

At last, the worm did turn. After a particularly pleasant evening for Anderson and Stevenson, a pleasure hardly shared by Clark, he conceived a most ingenious plan to confound his tormentors. O.W. had earlier been on the prowl, and Clark felt that it would be more than likely that a disturbance of any kind would bring him post-haste to quell it. It was quiet in the dormitory, where all but Clark were enjoying that first heavy sleep which is wont to fall upon both the just and the unjust. Clark sat up in bed, took a deep breath and began to give vent to the most ghastly cries of anguish.

'Anderson! Stevenson!' he shouted, 'stop it; you're hurting me. Help me!'

There was a gratifying stir below and slightly to the left, where O.W. was awaiting trouble expectantly in his study.

'Sir, come quickly,' continued Clark, really getting the feel of the part which he had chosen to play in this melodrama.

For such a large and elderly gentleman, O.W. moved with surprising speed. His thunderous steps were heard outside the door, and as he opened it, Clark repeated the names of those who were supposed to be harrying him – just in case the message had not got home. O.W. entered and put on the light. There was poor Clark in an obvious state of terror, and Stevenson was sitting up in bed, staring owlishly around him. There was, thought O.W., no need to mess around.

'I'll teach you,' he said, hauling Stevenson out by the scruff of the neck and administering a sharp dose of Attila.

Anderson had not yet woken up.

'Pretending, Anderson, are you?' called out O.W., and pulled him smartly into the correct beating position.

It was all over in a matter of seconds, and neither boy would have thought next morning that it was more than a painful dream if they had not collected a fine set of honourable scars to prove the reality of the incident. Strange to say, this dastardly action of Clark's was regarded as a point in his favour, and all three boys were bosom pals for the rest of the term.

And to Mike the end of the term did not seem long a'coming The last month simply flew by, what with exams and the Christmas party and the carol service. Though they grumbled exceedingly about the first of these three activities, the boys really looked forward to the exams. O.W. had a wonderful time organising them, turning the whole place upside down and Tony had an anxious week creating some sort of order out of the chaos.

The first sign of the upheaval which was about to take place was when O.W. asked for rough drafts of the papers He insisted on seeing every single sheet before duplicating began, and the more prudent had a set ready for his perusal They also made quite sure that they had copies, for some of the finest compositions in the past had been lost amids the general turbulence of O.W.'s desk, not to be rediscovered until long after the advertised time for the start of the exam in question. Flip Flap was caught out every single time, and there was never an end of term when she did not show extreme surprise that the time had come round for her to produce her masterpieces.

'Oh dear!' she would say, 'I haven't thought about what to set, and it really is so difficult. You see, I haven't finished the syllabus, the first form are so slow this term, and I don't know how far we'll have reached when the exams begin. And then there's the revising too; it's so hard to be fair when you know what questions you are going to ask.'

From time immemorial, this had been the burden of her song, and she was about to open her mouth in order to utter this sad lament, when it thundered forth from Topsy's direction before she could draw breath.

'That's what you said last term, Florence,' said Topsy at the end of the speech. 'I suppose it still holds good.'

It will be remembered that the secret of Topsy's little case had been let out at the firework display, when the tape recorder had received a severe, if glancing, blow. It so happened that the machine had been returned to Topsy after extensive repairs on the very morning of O.W.'s announcement about the exams. Unknown to everyone else, she had a tape of Flip Flap's effort of last term, and she felt that it might be amusing to try it out.

Flip Flap's look of bewildered amazement turned slowly into one of displeasure; her feelings were hurt, and she charged out of the room in a passion. So outraged was she that she spent a sleepless night concocting her papers, with the result that she handed them in two days before zero hour instead of her usual two days after it.

When the papers had been vetted, then came the duplicating. The school possessed a very reasonable typewriter and an up-to-date duplicator, and all but one of

151

the staff used them with fair success. Flip Flap, however, either scorned to use such things or else was too dumb to learn. She had not progressed beyond a hand-written effort and half a dozen sheets of carbon paper, so there was pandemonium in any room when the copies were presented to her pupils. The first four of each set were just legible, but woe betide the miserable boys who were presented with numbers five, six and seven. To make matters worse, the forms were so split up that there was a cross-section of the school in each room. O.W. did this with the laudable intention of stopping cribbing, but there was always a most gratifying improvement in the work of the smaller boys who had the good fortune to sit next to a kind-hearted member of the scholarship form. Having inspected the seating plan Mike had little hesitation in placing Duffield top of the third form Latin exam, for Anderson's ninety-seven per cent was so surprisingly ahead of current form that his intelligent neighbour must have had more than a hand in the improvement. Mike wondered whether the missing three per cent was due to carelessness or an artistic touch.

The very first exam caused more bad language than usual since Flip Flap was one paper short, had her pupils spread out in five different rooms and was supposed to be invigilating in one of them. She had to call in a substitute, and then tear into the other four rooms to find out who was short of a question paper. In each room, she was besieged with requests to interpret illegibilities, with the result that it took the whole school a good quarter of an hour to settle down to work.

At the end of the exam, there was an 'indignation meeting' in the staff room.

'I'm already a little tired of Flip Flap running around like a blue-arsed fly,' complained Hugh.

'You're second master, Tony,' said Ken. 'It's up to you to do something about it.'

'Single-handed, I can do very little. With a team of eager volunteers at my disposal, I am prepared to sort things out,' announced Tony.

Everyone volunteered to give up not more than half an hour of his time, and that evening all Flip Flap's remaining papers were confiscated. They were typed and duplicated, and the carbon copies were burnt, with the result that the remaining exams were carried out in a more orderly fashion.

The only other happening of note during the exams was when Ann thought that she had unmasked a cunning plot. There was, indeed, a very strong *prima facie* case against Golightly and Wilkinson. They had borrowed Clark's expensive periscope, and were seen cowering beneath the window of the duplicating room when Hugh was running off the Common Entrance form's maths papers. They were under grave suspicion, but their subsequent performance in the exam was such as to give credence to their story that they were investigating in secret the movements of a worm on the flower bed – rather than the nature of the questions which would be put in front of them the following Wednesday.

Exams safely over, the decorations were taken from their hiding-place, and Matron dressed ship for the end of term. Each piece, down to the mistletoe over O.W.'s study door, had its traditional place, which made the whole job far easier. Nelson, thought Matron, would never have slung his hammock in the main halyards, so there was no reason why Father Christmas on his sleigh should move from his correct place above the dining-room mantelpiece. The party consisted of silly games before a full Christmas dinner, the effects of which were lessened by a film show afterwards. All the staff had to wear paper hats throughout the proceedings, O.W.'s dunce's cap, Father Mirfield's mitre and Matron's naval cocked hat coming out, like the decorations, each year.

The final act of the term was a carol service in the church,

after which the school had truly broken up. It was really
against Father Mirfield's principles to have such a thing in
Advent, but he salved his conscience by announcing that
it wasn't really Christmas before the start of the service
and reminding his congregation at the end of it that they
were back in Advent. Advent hymns sung in darkness both
preceded and followed the glitter and lights of the carol
service. This, together with the fact that Father Mirfield
would put an extra 's' on Christmas whenever he wrote the
word, caused Matron's Protestant hackles to rise alarmingly.

'He's only been here a dog watch,' she was heard to
utter, 'and we've always had a carol service in the church
before breaking up.'

What is more, she made a point of going round after
him, and crossing out the offending 's' on notice-board,
on blackboard and in parish magazine.

So ended Mike's first term, and he and Ann were driven
down south by Ken, who had energetic but highly
uncomfortable plans for his own Christmas holiday. They
themselves were doing nothing very exciting, as they felt
that they should remain in the bosom of their families after
their first long absence from home. There would, of course,
be parties and dances and theatres, and they looked forward
to the break almost as eagerly as the stalwarts of the Common
Entrance form.

10

By the third week in January, there were few boys or staff who were not ready for the start of the Easter term. A very weather-beaten Ken collected Mike and Ann from their homes, and drove them back to Wintergreen in his battered old motor caravan. It was affectionately known as 'the White Spider', being named after a particularly unpleasant section of the notorious north face of the Eiger. In the past, it had taken Ken to the base of many mountains, waiting patiently at the bottom like a faithful hound until its master returned to collect it.

These holidays, the White Spider had been the means of transport and the temporary home of a two-man expedition attempting the first winter ascent of the north face of the comparatively unknown Himmelhorn. It was becoming increasingly difficult to find north faces which no one had previously succeeding in climbing in winter, and there were no fewer than seven other parties jockeying for position at the bottom when Ken and his French companion arrived on the scene. It may have been that the weather was so glorious that a winter climb was considered to be unsportingly pleasant by the others, or else that the Christmas festivities in the village of Glockenspiel were more attractive to them than they were to Mike and his partner. Anyway, the latter party moved off unobserved on Christmas Eve, and they weren't spotted until they were two-thirds of the way up the first of the long overhanging sections where 'artificial' climbing is necessary.

Climbers are fairly noisy, particularly when one of them

speaks good English and very broken French whilst the other's French is superb but whose English is confined to the coarser four-letter words pronounced astonishingly badly A noise was heard by one of the other climbers and, looking a long way upwards over the top of his tankard, he espied two tiny figures on the rock face, apparently in a spider's web of ropes, some white and some red. It took little time for the news to get around, Ken and Monsieur Jules Lesage hearing distinctly through the clear air the curses of their rivals in a variety of languages. The activity in the valley below was something terrific, as seven expeditions collected up themselves and their boots, their ropes, their pitons, their *étriers*, their krabs and all the other odds and ends which are essential for a climb of such severity.

The large American-Ukrainian party showed remarkable speed, and by the evening of the Feast of St Stephen was no more than a mere fifty feet below the leaders. However they were forced to cower beneath the last of the overhangs and watch half the mountainside sail past them, or they would have suffered the same sad fate as the martyr whose day it was. The Anglo-French expedition was scrambling up the last treacherous section before the summit and, though the American part of the pursuit ruled out malicious bombardment, the Ukrainians very definitely did not. In any case, Ken and Jules were feted on their return to the village (on Holy Innocents' Day), and their names will go down in climbing history.

All this was recounted by Ken on the way up north with becoming modesty, but there is no time to enlarge on the feat, or to relate the story of the second notable climb which followed. The eight parties, with the exception of the Ukrainians who were still sulking, combined to make a mass assault on the Matterhorn. The weather was perfectly frightful, and all of them thoroughly enjoyed themselves.

When they got back, Matron was in her usual rude health

and was delighted with her holiday hunting. One unfortunate hare had paid the supreme penalty for not looking where it was going, for it had completed its first circle with such devastating speed that it ran into the pack from the rear, and was unable to evade the gnashing jaws of the slower hounds. Matron was given a pad, which was greatly admired by the boys as it sat in a bottle of methylated spirits being pickled. According to her forecast, measles and chickenpox would make a clean sweep of those unticked on her lists, but there would be no mumps. To the fury of Hugh, she was absolutely right, and there were no matches the whole term. When the weather was right, which wasn't often, the germs were in full control.

It was gratifying to note that on St Stephen's Day, when Ken was battling upwards towards his goal, Hugh became the proud father of Stephen Golightly Twickenham Williams. Wilkinson won both the Common Entrance form sweepstake and kudos for his unerring calculations, whilst Golightly was enchanted to be chosen godfather of the infant prodigy. Hugh would have preferred a member of the first fifteen, but none of them was confirmed, so Golightly had to do. At the christening, held instead of a sermon on the first Sunday of the term, he took his duties very seriously, and he had more than was good for him of the champagne which Matron insisted on supplying at the festivities afterwards. Not being allowed to break the bottle over the baby's cot, she shared it out amongst the parents and godparents, but declined to drink any herself.

'Rotten stuff,' she announced, as she opened the second bottle, 'only fit for launchings. I've been drinking Stephen's health in Nelson's blood.'

From the first, Hugh maintained that his son had all the characteristics of an outstanding centre three-quarter, but O.W. favoured leader of the pack as his future role. His voice was certainly all right for that job, for he yelled enthusiastically whenever he liked, which did not always suit his father. Topsy took one recording of a disagreement between father and son at five o'clock in the morning. In spite of the fact that the sound effects were blanketed by the thickness of two intervening walls, the language of Williams *père* was both audible and appalling, with the result that the ladies on the staff were not invited to listen to the performance.

There were soon other annoyances for Hugh. The weather was cold, and the ground became too hard for rugger. Before the end of January, O.W. announced that Ingmere, a small lake about a mile away from Wintergreen, would shortly be capable of bearing the combined weight of the entire school. Then came a furious seeking of skates, with frenzied SOS messages by phone and letter to every part of the British Isles. Smythe, whose father was serving in the Middle East, even went so far as to send a request by air mail, though it was doubtful whether there was a pair of skates within a couple of thousand miles of the particular trouble spot where Major Smythe was stationed. Had his son required a couple of home-made bombs, he might have been able to oblige, he wrote a sharp letter back, reminding his firstborn that skates were not often needed when the temperature did not drop much below eighty in the shade. This reply did not, of course, arrive until a fortnight after the first expedition was made to the lake. Though Smythe himself was forced to borrow from more fortunate companions, there must have been nearly three-quarters of the school more or less suitably equipped. There was a wide variety of skates, ranging from Clark's extremely expensive modern pair to an antique couple of ancient blades set in wood, which must have been knocking about the school since the turn of the century. Anderson strapped these, with about seven feet of string, onto a pair of gym shoes, and it says much for the strength of his ankles that he managed quite nicely with them.

Of course, long before the great day, there had been slides, both legal and illegal. By a strange quirk of fate, it was the illegal ones, generally crossing a much-used path, which proved the more successful. There wasn't a member of the staff who wasn't inveigled onto these slides, even Flip Flap being persuaded to try out a short stretch which had been manufactured by the first form. Her frightened squeals were much appreciated, but she did not venture onto anything more advanced. The best slide of all was a semi-official one organised by Golightly, a slide which ran diagonally across the playground. Each night, it was watered with the aid of the fire hose, having been swept by its proprietor with loving care. It had been formally opened by Matron, who passed along its entire length with a grace and ease of motion reminiscent of a ship of the line under full sail gliding smoothly over calm seas.

'I christen this slide Golightly's,' she announced, 'and may all those who sail upon it reach port on an even keel.'

For some three days, all went well, but as always happened to slides at this particular spot, it met an unfortunate end. Mr Emmerson, the odd job man and husband to the cook, had occasion to cross the slide in the execution of his duties, and it was only a question of time before he landed on his keel with a jolt.

The inevitable catastrophe occurred one dark evening, just after the new surface had set nicely. When he had finished swearing and rubbing his hindquarters, the enraged Mr Emmerson sprinkled the slide with cinders, giving it a further watering so that they would set firmly and prevent Golightly from sweeping them off.

'Oh, Alf,' remonstrated his spouse, 'them boys does like it so. You didn't ought to 'ave done it.'

'Well, I 'ave, and if I catch that bloody Golightly, I'll do 'im,' was her consort's uncompromising rejoinder.

At last, the time came for the first trip to Ingmere, even

Mrs Willerby venturing out. When they all came to the shores of the lake, O.W. insisted on walking out alone upon the ice to test its strength. This was tradition, and a part of the proceedings which Mrs Willerby did not like. Her husband was a very heavy man and, if it never occurred to him that the ice might give way, it certainly occurred to her. She ran up and down the shore distractedly, like a mother hen in charge of a brood of ducklings. She feared that there would be a report like gunfire, followed by the total disappearance of the headmaster.

This performance had happened every skating season since their marriage, but there had never been the slightest cause for alarm, let alone an accident.

Ken was another pessimist, for he used to bring with him a variety of his climbing ropes, and there were festoons of grade-four nylon hanging from the branches of every convenient tree. Hugh was in the habit of laughing at him for this, saying that he was an old lady, which was odd in view of the fact that he called most of Ken's activities highly dangerous.

At a signal from O.W. that all was well, the school advanced onto the ice, some warily but most with a gay abandon. Considering that there were many novices in this larger section, it is hardly surprising that a good many feet shot from under their owners, and a good many bottoms hit the ice with a resounding thud. That afternoon, they were left to do as they pleased, but Hugh had already set his sights on a game of ice hockey. He felt this aimless expenditure of energy to be a complete waste of time, for it was beyond his comprehension that anyone could enjoy life unless he was within easy reach of a ball-like object, he challenged Mike to a race, feeling that some sort of competition was better than none, and in the ensuing contest he began to glow with self-satisfaction as he gradually drew ahead. Mike was no great skater, but it was nice to show one's superiority.

The smug smile, however, was soon wiped off Hugh's face when Topsy shot past him. Hands clasped behind his back and moving with no apparent effort, he was obviously several classes better than Hugh.

'I used to race in Norfolk,' he called, 'but I'm a little rusty now.'

'This is a private contest,' Hugh pointed out. 'There's no need for ruddy professionals to join in.'

He was still smarting when a small figure also shot by him in pursuit of Topsy. It was Clark in his expensive outfit, and it was quite clear that it was not wasted on him. Several luxurious winter holidays in Switzerland had been enjoyed by him, and he had made good use of the best coaching which money could provide.

'Well, I'll be damned!' announced Hugh, slowing down so that Mike could catch up with him. 'That is the final indignity. I'm going off to practise figures in a quiet corner.'

Hugh could not even be induced to join in a game of tag, which had just got going under Ann's instructions. In this, he was probably wise, for there seemed to be someone either fallen, about to fall or actually in the process of falling the whole time. Mike thoroughly enjoyed himself, until Matron pulled him aside, and engaged him in earnest conversation.

'Someone usually gets hurt by about this time,' she said.

'Oh, I don't know about that. They all seem to bounce quite nicely.'

'It's not that,' went on Matron. 'Have you ever seen a boy's hand when a skate's been over it?'

'I see your point,' said Mike. 'Shall I stop the game?'

'Not until someone loses a finger. You'll have to search the deck then for the missing joint. If it's discovered quickly, we can splice it on again.'

Somehow, the game didn't seem quite so attractive to Mike after this observation.

The next day, Hugh did organise a very rudimentary type of ice hockey, and was considerably narked when Clark put him right over certain minor points in the rules. The little wretch was quite an authority, but it was rather galling to have him laying down the law so firmly. However, Hugh had to admire his expert play, and by the end of the day he was almost prepared to grant him first-class citizenship on the strength of it.

There was a week or more of clear, cold weather, with skating every afternoon, and then came the snow. There are few small boys who do not lose all sense of proportion at the sight of the first snowflake, and almost before it has reached the ground they seem able to collect enough material for a fair-sized snowball. O.W. always started by being very lenient with them, and snowballing was seldom banned either before a window had been broken or before he himself had received an unexpected dollop down the back of his neck. Then there would be dire threats, and Attila would come into play if any boy so much as touched the snow.

This year, the first flakes began to fall shortly after midnight, and there was a foot or more of it upon the ground when the boys woke up. The first snowball was thrown by Stevenson two and a quarter minutes after the rising bell, the first window was broken just twenty-seven minutes after breakfast, and the first boy beaten at the beginning of break. Bedlam ceased as if by magic, and the usual fairly orderly routine quickly resumed. Snowballing, that is of the indiscriminate sort, was officially banned, but organised pitched battles instead of games were permitted. O.W. would probably have divided the school into two sides and let things rip, but Tony had invented a code of conduct which cut out a good deal of the punishment which can be inflicted on the unpopular or the foolhardy. It was an understood thing that there should be no rubbing, and that once a warrior was on the ground he could not be attacked.

In the afternoon, the first of these organised battles took place, a battle long remembered. O.W. and Matron were elected captains, with Hugh and Ken assisting the former, and Ann and Mike attached to the naval brigade. Flip Flap looked after the walking wounded who were not fighting, and Topsy insisted on taking his afternoon off. There were thirty-four on one side and thirty-five on the other. Rival headquarters were set up on either side of Dog Dyke, that meandering stream which figured prominently during the meet of the bassett hounds. Tony was the principal referee and he was aided by a couple of short-sighted seniors. Without their glasses they would be entirely useless to either side, and with them they would be dangerously accident-prone. Each, referee carried a whistle, the blowing of which caused an immediate ceasefire on both sides. It was explained that the whistles would be blown only in grave emergency, at a serious breach of the rules or when a point had been gained by either side.

Each base was thirty yards away from the Dyke, and was marked by a corner flag from the games equipment. Tethered to each flag by some twenty feet of cord were the respective captains, both suitably armoured against the cold which might assail them owing to their restricted movement. The object of the exercise was to hit the opposing captain with a snowball. Nothing below either knee or elbow counted, and it must be a direct hit clearly observed by one of the referees. This was quite a problem, for the existence of the stream made it difficult to close the range. Once in enemy territory, overwhelming odds might descend upon a lone attacker, and even on quite a strong assault party. If there was an attack *en masse*, a sudden light raid round their flank by a comparatively weak force might strike the first deadly blow. As soon as a captain had been hit, the whistles blew, a point was scored against the losing side and everyone had to return to base for a new throw-off.

Such were the rules of the tournament and, when all had been made clear to the combatants, action stations were taken up.

The battle opened according to plan, quite a textbook situation developing. Each captain disposed of the available forces in an orderly manner, with frontline troops, defenders whose role was to protect HQ at all costs and a mobile reserve ready to be rushed where danger threatened. For quite two minutes, there were volleys fired, O.W. calling 'Fire' and Matron calling 'Salvo' at approximately ten-second intervals. This was all very well for disciplined troops, but a little dull for Wintergreen irregulars. Soon, the volleys ceased and fighting became general, some aiming at their nearest foes, others taking optimistic long shots at enemy HQ. The defenders had little or no difficulty in protecting their captains, and neither side was as yet forced to retire from forward positions on the dyke side.

It may have been thought transference, but Ken and Mike recollected the Battle of Hastings at approximately the same moment. Both of them decided that there was little future in this type of warfare, and that the trajectory must be radically altered if a quick blow was to be struck. In order to achieve a positive result, both girded up their loins and hurled their missiles an unprecedented height into the still air. No one took the least interest in their actions, for the attackers had no time to pause and admire the efforts of friend or foe, and the defenders were gazing ahead, prepared to parry any blow which looked like reaching their HQ. Little did they appreciate that nemesis was descending upon their respective champions, and the throwers themselves, having as it were drawn a bow at a venture, did not realise how successful their efforts were going to be. At exactly the same moment, the two descending missiles reached their targets, two whistles blew and two blaspheming commanding officers rubbed the snow off their faces and shoulders. The score was one all.

This manoeuvre was one which could not possibly be repeated. Matron unfurled an immense golfing umbrella, which she had brought specifically for such an occasion and had forgotten to use; O.W. was presented with an old dustbin lid by one of his retainers, and stood like some ancient Chinese mandarin protected from both mortar fire and passing birds. Fresh tactics were required, and it is interesting to note that, whilst O.W. favoured the thin red line, Matron employed the strategy which had brought undying glory to her hero, Lord Nelson.

O.W.'s men lined the bank, their flanks unturnable since they stretched into the middle distance, but Matron organised her fleet in such a manner that an immense concentration of fire was directed at one spot, a spot which presented a possible crossing. Here she intended to break the enemy's line.

Suddenly, a powerful squadron was over, and formed up in arrowhead formation upon the further bank. Golightly was at the apex and, on the given command, they all about turned. Golightly's broad stern made a perfect target, and attracted a withering fire as the formation advanced backwards towards the enemy base. Matron felt that she had no historical precedent for sending an entire flotilla in to the attack going full astern, but she was always prepared to improvise if the occasion demanded it. Crouching low, and protected by the shield of advancing bottoms, Duffield acted as a kind of cox, guiding his vessel, like the six hundred, apparently into the valley of death. The metaphors are considerably mixed, but so was the situation.

O.W.'s defenders and mobile reserve did their best, and even some of the thin red line deserted their forward positions, but all were utterly confounded by the novelty of the situation. When the backing troops could be expected to see the whites of O.W.'s eyes, they were given the order to turn by Duffield.

'Starboard broadside,' called out Matron, and a deadly rain of shot scattered the last of the opposition.

'Port broadside,' she shouted, only just giving them time to transfer their spare snowballs to their throwing arms.

It was virtually impossible to miss, and a swift blast of the whistle proclaimed that Matron's side was leading by two hits to one.

By this time, the terrain had become considerably cut up, and by mutual arrangement the battlefield shifted upstream. O.W. elected to set up his standard on a peninsula, surrounded on three sides by the dyke. The great Duke of Wellington himself could hardly have picked on a better position.

'Suits us all right,' said Matron. 'We'll blockade them. They're scuppered already.'

Thereupon, she spread her forces evenly round the bend, and prepared to mete out severe punishment. O.W., however, was an old campaigner. Not only had he interior lines of communication, but he had also taken possession of a magnificent strong point at the tip of the peninsula. There he had noticed both a plentiful supply of ammo and very effective cover. By placing a strong section at this forward position, he could enfilade the enemy. Matron's forces were in receipt of a most uncomfortable crossfire, and it would be enormously difficult to dislodge the enemy. Matron was most upset that she had not got her side into this strategic position first.

It was Ann who suggested a method of smoking out the hornet's nest and, after a hurried council of war, preparations were started in the dim distance. An enormous snowball was begun, and gradually rolled towards the brink of a bank protecting the outpost. The larger it became, the more cover it provided, and more and more of Matron's side were seconded from other duties to provide motive power for this engine of war.

Ken, who saw nothing of the approach of this menace, was gratified to notice the enemy melting away, but continued to direct enfilading attacks on anyone who remained within range. He took the shouts of warning which O.W. was giving him as encouragement to continue his efforts. The snowball was really colossal and, when it was no more than three feet from the heads of Ken and his men, the chief referee decided that someone would be killed in the avalanche, he blew his whistle, and action ceased along the whole front.

'That snowball must not be moved,' called out Tony.

'Why not, sir?' asked Duffield. He and his friends had put enormous energy into the project, and he was indignant.

'Too dangerous, Duffield,' pronounced the referee, amidst cries of 'Oh no, sir' from Matron's supporters and 'Oh yes, sir' from O.W.'s.

'What a referee! You might have decided that before we had used up so many calories, sir,' said Duffield.

'What's a calory, Duffer?' asked his fat friend.

Meanwhile, Ken moved from his position under the lee of the bank. He was quite unnerved by the sight of the danger which threatened.

'Well, I, for one, appreciate Mr Coleridge's ruling,' he said with feeling.

A confused bickering was broken up by the naval commander.

'Pipe down, there,' she shouted. 'I have a proposition to make. We won't use our ship-to-shore missile, but Mr Padgett and his flotilla must take no further part in the engagement.'

'Nonsense, Matron,' answered O.W. 'You were employing unfair tactics.'

'And why, may I ask? Miss Pinkerton's plan was brilliantly

conceived and executed. The operation was perfectly legitimate.'

Golightly was a little puzzled by this; he thought that the term applied exclusively to babies.

'But it was unsafe, Matron,' said Tony, sticking to his point. 'Your secret weapon must weigh the best part of a ton.'

'Well, we certainly made an engineering job of it, Mr Coleridge, if that's what you mean.'

'You'd have jolly well squashed us, Matron,' broke in Ken.

'And that, Mr Padgett, is exactly why you should consider yourself scuppered,' finished Matron triumphantly.

'I claim a hit on Matron for dangerous play,' announced O.W. He had just seen something out of the corner of his eye which made it essential that the argument should continue unabated for a short while longer.

'No, repetition no,' said Matron with great emphasis, employing the most forceful negative in her repertoire. 'We are being unduly penalised. Mr Padgett puts himself on a lee shore, and then wonders why he is in danger.'

'May I make a suggestion?' asked Mike at last.

'I suppose so,' said Matron and O.W. together.

'Delighted to hear it,' said Tony, who had obviously a higher opinion of Mike's powers as a plenipotentiary than the rival commanders.

'Well, our side doesn't touch the snowball again, but Mr Padgett's patrol is forced to withdraw – his position is untenable.'

'Oh, very well. I'll agree to that,' said Matron.

'That's all very well,' said O.W. 'I am willing to withdraw to prepared positions, but not with that snowball perched where it is. Most of Matron's side could hide behind it; I should never have consented to this choice of site if I had foreseen that such unfair artificial cover was going to be put in position.'

'Very well,' said Matron quickly. 'We'll roll it over the bank.'

It must be admitted that her gracious consent was not all that magnanimous, for she had suddenly seen that the descent of the abandoned missile into the bed of the dyke could be used to her advantage. It might well create a bridge over which another arrowhead formation might be flung. The snowball, accordingly, was pushed to the brink, and crashed down to the accompaniment of cheers on both sides. Tony, and perhaps even more than him, Ken were very glad that nobody had been in the way of its downward path. The whistle sounded for the reopening of hostilities, and a plan for a further sweep into enemy waters was quickly mounted by Matron.

But it never came off.

When the giant snowball was at the start of its career, no bigger indeed than a football, Hugh Williams and a chosen band of members of the first fifteen, mostly forwards, had withdrawn from the field of battle. They had escaped unobserved, crossed the dyke and started on a great circle of which even the Wintergreen hare would have been proud. During the negotiations over the future conduct of the war, they had completed their encircling movement, for O.W. had spotted them, and had managed to keep the discussion going whilst they took up positions behind a hedge not fifty yards from the naval HQ. So complete was the surprise that they could easily have come stealthily out of their hiding place, walked up to Matron and torpedoed her before one single member of her force was a penny the wiser. What did happen was possibly more spectacular – and there was no difference in the final result.

Hugh and his men sprang forth with bloodcurdling yells, and charged with all the élan expected of first fifteen forwards. It would be untrue to say that Matron panicked, though she considered that discretion was the better part of valour and backed away from the onslaught. Her defenders turned to meet this totally unexpected threat and, being closer to her than were the enemy, managed to come to her aid. In order to make a human wall between their gallant commanding officer and the foe, they charged past her, but they quite forgot one thing. Matron was tethered to the flag by a piece of cord, now stretched taut in her anxiety to put as much sea room as possible between herself and danger. It only required the leader of the rescue party to trip over the cord, and the rest of them fell over him. An already disorganised defence had now reached disintegration point.

'I'm slipping my cable,' said Matron, as she felt herself being drawn into the vortex of writhing defenders, but long before she had performed that feat, the whistles announced beyond all manner of doubt that she had received a number of direct hits.

The score was now two all and, in view both of the late hour and the fact that tempers were slightly frayed, Tony called it a day. Though arguments as to the legality of Hugh's encircling movement during a truce went on until the end of the term, and were even started again during the summer, a draw seemed to be the only fair result.

The term dragged on, and even the boys grew a little tired of the snow. There were incidents in plenty, but it is time to proceed to the end of term. Owing to the vagaries of the golden number and the paschal moon, Easter was very early that year. This being so, Father Mirfield had persuaded O.W. to hang on to his charges until the feast was over. A satisfactorily gloomy Lent was interspersed with services of a colourful nature, perhaps the most exhilarating being on the evening of Holy Saturday. During a ceremony which Matron insisted that not one of the apostles themselves would have recognised as even vaguely Christian, every light in the church was put out. It was the duty of Tony and the butcher, the two MCs, to kindle a symbolic flame, a kind of minor bonfire, in the porch, from which fire was taken to light every candle. It was an impressive ceremony, very much appreciated by the boys, all of whom had candles, but was somewhat marred by the ejaculations of the butcher, whose handlebars were once more in danger of destruction. As Matron said to Father Mirfield afterwards:

'You spikes are all the same. You alter the ritual just when it suits you. I'm sure that last year we didn't have "Mind my bloody moustache" in response to "Let there be light".'

She was quite right. Last time, it had been 'Where's the flaming extinguisher?' as the conflagration looked like getting out of hand.

Towards the end of term, there had been sessions of instruction for the Lake District party. Ken had briefed his charges on Youth Hostel routine and safety rules on the fells. He had told them how to keep both themselves and the wardens happy at the hostels; he had emphasised that in order to love the mountains they had also to respect them. Not one of the boys could complain that he had not been warned of every single complication which could arise, and they were commanded to be in good training for the venture.

11

'Well, here we are,' said Ken, as the White Spider drew up in Patterdale.

It had been an interesting trip from Wintergreen, where the Lake District party had assembled the previous evening. They had started off before eight o'clock that morning, and had reached the shores of Ullswater in time for a picnic lunch. Duffield, of course, had been instrumental in getting them there in one piece, having done everything except actually drive the car. From the way that he laid down the law, one would never have guessed that his father worked for British Rail, and the family took great pride in neither possessing a car nor even entering one unless it was strictly necessary. Macpherson had surprised the whole lot of them by his astounding knowledge of cars. He, who knew so little about anything else (apart from games), could tell at a glance the make of every car and lorry on the road; he could give full details of the model, from year of manufacture to current value on the second-hand market, and, with his eyes shut, he could generally tell from the noise of the engine what kind of car was approaching. On two occasions, he was tested, and was extremely disappointed that he could do no better than guess seven correct makes of car out of ten each time.

'You see, it's my hobby,' he explained modestly when everyone showed surprise at his erudition, 'and Dad does keep a large garage. By the way, sir, this clutch of yours won't last all that much longer.'

'Could you repair it for me, Mac?'

172

'Yes, sir. I'd get the parts from Dad, but it would cost quite a bit.'

He gave a quotation which subsequently proved very much cheaper than that of the garage which normally coped with the ailments suffered by the ageing White Spider. Macpherson got the job, and Ken had no cause to regret it. As he said afterwards, he often learnt rather more about a boy after ten days in the Lake District than during his whole school career.

The boys could not look at the water for very long before they started to throw stones. There is always the risk that someone will get wet on these occasions, and it was Anderson who sat down heavily in two inches of water.

'Oh, sir, can I change my bags?'

'No, they can darned well dry on you. We'd better get cracking.'

'There's a nice breeze blowing, and you won't be uncomfortable for long,' said Ann kindly.

'Please, sir, can we go up Helvellyn?' asked Stevenson.

He had been given the detailed programme for the entire trip, complete with wet weather alternatives, and a rather more modest start to the tour had been planned. Stevenson, however, had a one-track mind, and Helvellyn was very much uppermost in it.

'No,' said Ken. 'We'll take our time over Helvellyn – but you'll be able to see our route all right from the top of Place Fell.'

Place Fell was on the other side of the lake, a fine two thousand-footer, and just the thing for the first afternoon. Within ten minutes of Anderson's unfortunate little accident, the Wintergreen invasion of the mountains had begun. The party crossed Goldrill Beck by the bridge, pausing to see whether there were any trout on view. There were no fish in sight, so Stevenson and Anderson thought fit to indulge in a short spitting competition. Soon, however, they were on the path which leads to Boardale Hause, the local Piccadilly Circus for walkers in that area.

'Ah, a seat,' said Golightly, sprinting very creditably ahead so that he could rest for a short while upon an iron bench which was somewhat surprisingly awaiting the weary traveller.

'That's no way to climb, Golly,' said Duffield severely. 'You must produce a nice steady rhythm, or we'll never get you to the top.'

'Let him learn for himself, Duffer,' said Ken.

All went well, except that Anderson would keep shooting ahead and, when he came to any dividing of the ways, he shouted back for guidance.

'Which way, sir?' he yelled on three separate occasions, but no one took the least notice of him. Finding it quite impossible to wait, he chose his own route and, being a poor guesser, found himself three times at the tail of the line instead of in the lead.

'The points are always wrong for you,' said Mike.

'You might tell me when I'm going wrong, sir,' said Anderson. 'It takes me ages to get back onto the right path.'

Quite a long time later, when several legs were feeling a little weary, there were enquiries of an agonised nature.

'How much more, sir?' asked Golightly. 'This mountain is very high.'

'It's only just over two thousand feet – we'll be near the three thousand feet mark tomorrow,' answered Ken, which gave several of the party food for thought.

'Please, sir,' asked Wilkinson, 'how high are we now?'

'One thousand seven hundred and fourteen feet,' answered Mike promptly. They were more like two thousand, having left Boardale Hause far below them, but Wilkinson seemed quite happy with the answer. Duffield was a little way behind, doing interesting things with a compass and a one-inch map, or he would not have let the inaccuracy pass.

Soon the summit cairn hove in sight, and there wasn't a boy who didn't put on a spurt. Anderson was still in the lead, and he reckoned that he touched the winning post a fraction before Macpherson.

'Please, sir, I was first, wasn't I?'

'Yes, by a short finger – but does it matter all that much?' asked Mike.

'Very much – to him,' said the first man to climb the north face of the Himmelhorn in winter.

It was a glorious April afternoon, so they were able to look around without shivering and wanting to get off the tops as quickly as possible. From their vantage point, they could be shown just what was in store for them during the next few days.

'There's High Street, where we're going tomorrow,' said Ken, and he traced their route past Angletarn Pikes and the Knott.

'Funny name for a mountain,' said Wilkinson.

'It's got a Roman road on it...' started Duffield, delighted at the thought of giving a short lecture on the subject.

'It looks a very long way,' broke in Golightly, to whom the laws of gravity applied particularly severely.

'Oh, it's not too bad at all. A bit of a grind at times, but easy going all the way – there's nothing like Striding Edge,' said Ken, turning towards Helvellyn.

Some four miles from them was that formidable barrier, looking particularly delectable to Stevenson.

'Please, sir,' he asked, 'can't we go up tomorrow?'

'No, we'll stick to High Street but, weather permitting, it will be Thursday.'

'But, sir, what happens if it's wet?'

'We'll delay the climb for a day, and nip up on Friday before we move off to Eskdale.'

'Thank you, sir,' said Stevenson. Life would never be quite the same again if he didn't reach the top, and he was relieved to hear that there could be a second bite at the cherry.

A sudden cooling gust of wind reminded them that it was time to move. Instead of retracing their steps, Ken led them straight on, with Ullswater on their left. They lost height all the time, eventually reaching a lakeside path very highly praised by the guide book. It should be stated here that Ken invariably carried close to his heart the appropriate volume of *A Pictorial Guide to the Lakeland Fells,* by A. Wainwright. Though he did not always share the author's views, he respected them, and he admitted that if he wandered over the District for the next forty years he would still not be as knowledgeable as the great Mr Wainwright.

A halt for light refreshment out of Ken's rucksack was made at Silver Bay. Before the last boy had been supplied, there were stones skimming across the surface of the waters, but operations were suspended when Anderson had the misfortune to slip once more and had to be wrung out. Smythe, who has not yet been mentioned during the trip, made an entry in the notebook which he was carrying somewhat ostentatiously.

'What are you doing, Smig?' asked Golightly.

'Writing my journal, Golly.'

'Well, tell us what you've said.'

'Nice tea by Ullswater. Anderson fell in.'

'Is that all?'

'No, I've got – "Climbed Place Fell (2154 feet) after nice dinner by Ullswater. Anderson fell in." '

'Do you hear that, Stinker?' called out Mike. 'You're mentioned twice in the official diary already.'

'Please, sir, it wasn't my fault, sir. I slipped,' said Anderson, who felt this to be a good and reasonable excuse.

It should be mentioned that in those days cars were frowned upon at Youth Hostels, and that they were going to the old Goldrill House, not the luxury hostel now awaiting the tired traveller. They all trooped back to the White Spider, and from the compartment in the rear collected their goods and chattels. The short trek to the hostel took them past two hotels, the one on the right and the other on the left, which caused Golightly to remark conversationally:

'I suppose you'll be boozing tonight. I hope you staff won't all get drunk.'

'Probably "yes" and certainly "no",' answered Ken, who was always careful to choose hostels within reach of licensed premises. He found looking after the young very thirsty work.

As now, hostels opened their hospitable doors promptly at five o'clock in the evening, and shut them very firmly at ten o'clock the next morning. It was, however, well after six when the party booked in, and supper was at seven o'clock. Before then, there had to be some frantic unpacking and making up of beds. Blankets had to be wrestled with, for this was long before the days of the ubiquitous duvet. Anderson and Stevenson decided to pool their resources, which meant that the blankets did not have it entirely their own way, but even then Mike decided that at some time during the night both of them would be effecting necessary repairs. The menfolk were accommodated in the attic dormitory, where there were already several other hostellers installed, and Ann found herself in a room containing two middle-aged spinsters. They gave no details of their past lives, though it was obvious that they were schoolmarms of some kind. They seemed amused by the Wintergreen boys, but stated that they were heartily thankful that they were not 'in loco parentis'.

It was agreed by all that it was a very good supper. Surely, no Youth Hostel meal can be anything but very tasty after even half a day on the fells. Then it was time to relax, for another party was doing the washing-up and all were free immediately after the meal.

'What's the staff doing, sir?' asked Duffield.

'Need you ask? A chap of your intelligence should know.'

'Consuming alcohol on licensed premises, I presume, sir.'

'Yes, in the interests of science, we must test the specific gravity of the beer,' answered Ken.

'Can we have a look round, sir?'

'By all means, Duffield,' said Ken, adding as an afterthought, 'you might pass it around though that I am not particularly fond of faces peering in at me through the bar window.'

'I shall personally see that you are not interfered with, sir,' said Duffield in his gentleman's gentleman voice.

As they were going down to the pub, Mike asked Ken whether it was wise for no one to be on duty.

'You've got to trust them, and our lads have never let me down badly. Anyway, the warden is the real boss at a hostel. All the same, I shan't be staying long on the first night.'

'That little twerp Anderson will probably be in the river before you're back,' said Ann.

'Well, he's quite a good swimmer,' said Mike.

'If he gets wet again, he goes to bed and stays there,' said Ken.

Actually, Duffield had already ordered him to bed when Ken returned to the hostel twenty minutes later, and Smythe did not hesitate to make the usual entry in his log.

'You seem a little accident-prone, Andy,' said Ken.

'It wasn't my fault, sir. I slipped,' was the plaintive reply from a top bunk.

Anderson's clothes were more or less dry the next morning, so the wind soon completed the job on the way to High Street, the day's objective.

Mike and Ann stayed on at the pub for another half hour. They discussed the events of the day and the prospect for the rest of the holiday.

'Well, we all got up Place Fell all right,' said Mike, 'but
the programme seems on the tough side for the boys.'

'I'd agree with you if Ken hadn't run these trips before.
He says that the kids can do a man's day, provided that
they don't have to hump too much around.'

'What are they going to be like at the end of the trip?'

'Probably very fit and certainly very dirty.'

'Anyway,' went on Mike, 'Ken seems to be quite safe.
He won't stay on the tops with them if the weather turns
nasty.'

'He knows his stuff, but I still don't like them not wearing
boots.'

'Oh, there's something to be said for fell shoes; I might
be converted. I wore mine, and my feet feel fine tonight.'

'Well, you won't get me wearing them,' said Ann firmly.

'You're an old stick-in-the-mud. Will you let our children
wear them, or put them in socking great hobnails at the
age of two?'

'We haven't got any children, Mike.'

'I know we haven't – I was assuming that we might in
due course.'

'There are some formalities to be gone through first, you
know.'

'What? Oh, yes, would you like me to propose to you?'

'Not in the public bar, it's undignified.'

'Then come on outside; we've finished our beer.'

'What a very romantic approach, Mike!'

'I'm sorry, perhaps there'll be a moon awaiting us.'

There was a moon all right, but it cast its romantic light
upon Golightly and Smythe as well as upon the prospective
lovers. It seemed uncivil to tell them to get stuffed when
they attached themselves firmly as escorts, since they so
obviously felt that they were lending tone to the party. It
was not until the troops had been packed off to bed, and
Ken had volunteered to stay around, that Mike and Ann

179

could be alone. They walked to the bridge, and leant over it. Mike put his arm round Ann, but he was unable to start saying what he wanted to say before she spoke.

'No, Mike, please don't,' she said. 'I want you to think very hard before you ask me to marry you.'

'But I have.'

'Well, please just think again. We've been knocking about together for years now, and I should like it to go on and on, but we're both still very young.'

'I've made up my mind to marry you, you know.'

'Yes, Mike, and I'm all for it – in time. But would we be any happier if we were officially engaged now?'

'I don't see why not.'

'It's bound to be a very long engagement, and that's not always a good thing.'

'Undergraduates have been known to marry.'

'No, Mike, it won't do. I want a year or two as a policewoman – without a husband – whilst you're at the university.'

'OK, if you want it that way. It suits me.'

'But will it if we are engaged? I'm not so sure whether it's fair on either of us, but I couldn't turn you down on the strength of that. Please don't ask me to marry you before you've really chewed it over for a few days.'

'Right, I'll chew,' said Mike, and he kissed her.

'Bet you I can spit further than you,' said Ann as soon as she was able to say anything, and there was yet another contest over the bridge.

Wednesday dawned fair, but there was something about the weather which Ken distrusted.

'You can risk it if you like,' he told the party, 'but I'm taking waterproofs.'

All of them had some sort of wet weather gear to don over their anoraks, but Golightly was the only boy to take his. Duffield had originally planned to keep him company, but he had the erroneous idea that one of the adults might carry the wet-weather gear for him. After all, the packed meals were in a rucksack, and his waterproof cape would hardly be noticed. When he learnt that he would have to carry it himself, he had no hesitation in joining the foolish virgins of the expedition, Mike also risked it, but Ann was equipped for the very worst kind of weather.

The ascent was uneventful, and can be covered adequately by the entry in Smythe's journal. Possibly owing to the spelling of his own name, he was a little apt to add an 'e' to certain words, but the original text is intelligible:

Hade sandwiches on tope of High Street (2718 feet). Swapped my corned dog sandwich for a super egg and cheese one. Stopped at Angle Tarn, but Anderson did not fall in because Miss Pinkerton sate on him. Saw four deer in distance, and one of them hade horns. Kenny said it must of been a stage. Snow on tope near wall, views *tres bon*.

The glory of the day had somewhat departed by the end of the meal, but the party moved onwards. The clouds were close to their heads, and the carriers of waterproof extras began to feel that they might be needed after all. The boys were a little upset that there was nothing very Roman about the path which they followed. This did not prevent them from making Latin noises under the guidance of Duffield. On hearing that the VIPs would have been carried in a litter by slaves, Anderson was hoisted on their shoulders and borne in triumph for the best part of a hundred yards before the slaves got tired of him and dropped him. Luckily, they chose a level stretch and not a precipice – so he was probably luckier than more than one unpopular traveller in Gallo-Roman times.

They lost height very gradually, and then started to climb again as they swung to the right.

'Oh dear, oh dear,' moaned Golightly, 'why do we have to go up again?'

'This is nothing, we'll soon be on the top, and it's a new summit for your collection,' said Mike.

'What's it called, sir?' asked Smythe, mentally licking his pencil in anticipation of a further entry in the journal.

'Thornthwaite Crag (two thousand five hundred and sixty-nine feet),' broke in Duffield promptly.

'And that cairn on top is just about the finest I've ever seen,' went on Ken. 'You couldn't very well mistake it for any other in the Lake District.'

At this moment, the mist descended, rose momentarily and then came down again. The expedition seemed to be in the middle of damp cotton wool.

'Keep together,' shouted Ken, and he had a quick count to make sure that none of his flock had strayed.

'What a swizz!' said Stevenson, thinking that the trip up Helvellyn on the morrow might be in jeopardy.

'Don't you worry,' said Anderson consolingly. 'Sir's not going to get lost.'

Duffield's compass was out in a flash.

'Steer north-west, sir, and we'll be all right.'

'Thank you, navigator, a touch more to starboard, I fancy,' replied Ken.

They were soon congregated round the cairn, a truly magnificent beacon over twelve feet high, and Ken made a hasty change of plan. He had originally decided to walk northwards, along Grey Crag, a narrow ridge commanding excellent views. There were steep cliffs on either side, and no guiding wall ran along the top, but only a congenital idiot could have gone far astray. On the other hand, there was now nothing to see outside a depressing circle perhaps

182

wenty yards across, and there was a perfect escape route
o lower ground.

'We'll make for Threshthwaite Cove,' he announced.
Keep close together; here's a wall which we follow, and we
ught to be out of the mist in five minutes.'

Actually, it was a little longer, for the clouds were coming
down all the time, and Golightly had the misfortune to trip
up over his own feet and land on his nose. It was very lucky
hat he had the good sense to choose the only piece of
og on the entire hillside, and the main damage was done
o his dignity. He was picked up tenderly and felt for broken
ones, but was none the worse after the mud had been
craped out of his eyes.

'For God's sake, look where you're going,' said Ken rather
harply. 'We'd have had to carry you down on a stretcher
f you'd landed on rock.'

Some of the party looked very thoughtful at this, but the
ension was broken by Wilkinson.

'Couldn't have done himself much harm, sir. Golly's
ead's the toughest thing about him – he'd have split the
ocks.'

'Well, don't test it out,' said Ken. 'It's bad for my nerves.'

The pass above Threshthwaite Cove is a wild spot. They
vere just below the level of the clouds, so they could see
he slope down which the Roman road had run diagonally
n its way to Ambleside. In the distance was Windermere,
t the end of the narrow valley, and Troutbeck Tongue
tood out curiously. However, they soon turned their backs
n the scene, and tramped down towards the other valley
vith the wind behind them.

'How's the time going?' asked Mike.

'Not three yet. We've a couple of hours to fill in before
he hostel opens.'

'Blast!'

'Yes, and you're going to get wet,' said Ann a little too

cheerfully for Mike's comfort. As she spoke, she pulled
towel out of her rucksack, and wrapped it carefully roun
her neck.

It wasn't raining much yet, only a slight drizzle, but ther
was an ominous finality about it which was somewha
depressing to those without waterproofs. It took them ove
half an hour to reach the village of Hartsop, by which tim
the drizzle was no longer slight.

'We'll have tea in the bus shelter,' said Ken, and he le
his troops towards the main road.

'It's rather fun walking in the rain,' said Golightly somewha
tactlessly to Mike. He was enveloped in waterproof legging
and cape, and on his head was a formidable sou'wester.

'You'd look better with a socking great fish over you
shoulder,' said Mike sourly, thinking of that well-know
advertisement for cod liver oil.

The sanctuary of the bus shelter was reached befor
anyone was really soaked, but they arrived there in the nic
of time. The drizzle turned into a steady downpour as th
chocolate was taken out and divided.

'Is this all we get, sir?' asked Macpherson. He was a ver
big boy with the voracious appetite of a shark, and it seeme
to him an incredibly long time since he had polished o
his own packed meal and all the leftovers which his fussie
companions had rejected. The tea was an ounce of chocolat
and a couple of biscuits, designed merely to stave o
starvation temporarily.

'We don't want to spoil your appetite for supper,' sai
Ann.

'But, Miss Pinkerton, this wouldn't satisfy a flea.'

'Then you'd better spend your pocket money on a privat
supply of nourishing food if you can't last out on this.'

'Yes, Miss Pinkerton,' said Macpherson, and Ann wondere
why he should have looked so very awkward.

As a matter of fact, he had already invested the half crow

hich Ken was in the habit of doling out after breakfast
ach morning in a packet of cigarettes. He liked a quiet
uff from time to time, but had the good sense not to be
oo blatant about it.

'How far off is the hostel, sir?' asked Duffield, after they
ad spent some twenty minutes in their retreat.

'Not more than a couple of miles. We'll wait here for a
it longer so that those who were not prudent enough to
ring the proper gear don't have to hang around sopping
ie other end.'

'Is the drying-room adequate, sir?'

'More than adequate, Duffield, it's excellent – and you
ill be badly in need of its services.'

'An idea has occurred to me, sir.'

'Oh, and what's that?'

'We could avoid taking up so much space in the drying-
oom, sir. It would, in fact, be public spirited.'

'How?'

'I feel a little diffident about mentioning it, sir, but you
re well-clad for this weather – and you could collect us in
ie White Spider.'

'I see what you mean,' said Ken, who was beginning to
el bored, 'but it is really against the rules – hostel rules
you know.'

'I sometimes feel,' said Duffield, 'that one is justified in
ompounding a felony.'

'For once, my dear Duffer, I am inclined to agree with
ou,' said Ken – and a felony was compounded.

Ann and Golightly moved off after Ken with an aggravating
vagger, whilst Mike stayed with the other foolish virgins
1 the bus shelter. He would like to have been rude to the
escue party, since their air of superiority was irksome to
im. Smythe had been writing up his journal and, when
e put it back in his pocket, he felt a tennis ball in its inner
ecesses. It was seldom that he separated himself from such

185

a treasure (there is always someone like him in every schoo
party), and its appearance was welcomed by all. The nex
half hour was passed very pleasurably in an interesting gam
thought up on the spur of the moment, so the time passe
more quickly than Mike had dared to hope. Their transpo
carried them safely back to Patterdale, and they were abl
to pass through the hostel doors on the stroke of five.

'Somebody's stolen one of my shoes,' complained Golight
in the drying-room next morning.

'Did you tie them together as Mr Padgett told you?' aske
Mike, who happened to be there too.

'I forgot, sir.'

'Well, never mind. You'd probably have lost both of ther
if you had.'

'But what shall I do, sir?'

'Go on rummaging, or you'll have to hop all the wa
today.'

After a few minutes, there was a cry of triumph, an
Golightly retired joyfully. Duffield then came in to colle
his property. He searched diligently.

'Please, sir. Somebody's stolen one of my shoes,' he sai
at last.

'There must be a thief about. Golightly had the sam
trouble only a couple of minutes ago, but the proble
solved itself.'

A prolonged search did produce another shoe of th
correct size, but unfortunately both shoes fitted Duffield
left foot and there was no name in either.

'Were your shoes marked, Duffield?'

'Oh, I think so, sir.'

'Well, I don't, but you've made some progress,' said Mik
cheerfully. 'Now go and look for someone with two rig
feet.'

Duffield carried out a very thorough inspection. Macpherson had gigantic feet, whilst both Anderson's and Stevenson's shoes were so minute that Duffield knew that he must seek elsewhere. Wilkinson and Smythe took more or less the same size, but they possessed perfectly matching pairs. They removed their right shoes, not entirely without objection, and displayed their initials in smudgy letters on the inside of the canvas. This narrowed things down considerably.

'Right,' said Duffield, 'where's that Golightly?'

He found him at last in the dining-hut, looking puzzled and disheartened.

'I say, Duffer,' he said, 'one of these shoes seems to have shrunk a little; it's damned uncomfortable.'

'Golly, you are a clot. Can't you see you've got two right shoes?'

'Have I? That accounts for it, it's a nuisance.'

'And I've got two left shoes.'

'Oh, Duffer, that makes a pair of us. It's bad; what can we do?'

'Just nip along, and ask Mr Padgett for instructions,' said Duffield, adding quietly to himself, 'this is going to be fun.'

It was not until Golightly was halfway through a detailed explanation of the phenomenon, in front of the whole party, that the penny dropped, after which a ceremonial exchange of shoes took place amidst ribald remarks.

'That wasn't fair, Duffer,' complained his friend, 'you know I'm just a little bit thick.'

'As thick as two short planks,' said Mike cruelly, 'but we like you for it.'

It was still raining, so poor Stevenson was in a terrible state. He had asked *ad nauseam* whether it was going to be fine, starting at seven o'clock, when talking was permitted but not encouraged. Twice he had poked his head through the skylight to inspect the weather, with the result that Macpherson's bed did not escape a small cascade each time.

187

'Please, sir,' he asked for the umpteenth time, 'is it goin
to clear?'

'I rather think that it will,' replied Ken, though to everyon
else there seemed small grounds for such optimism.

As they trudged off, Golightly started to grumble.

'Can't think what sir's doing. Surely we aren't going u
in this.'

Clad in his seafaring costume, he walked through Patterdal
uttering pronouncements of which Cassandra herself woul
have been proud. Ken dawdled, encouraging his protégé
to loiter at the shops. He was playing for time, for he fe'
that it must have just about rained itself out. His luck held
for by the time that the turning up to Helvellyn was reachec
the drizzle had ceased. Stevenson, who up until this momer
had been mourning, began to look a little less desolate.

'Please, sir, it is going to clear, isn't it?' he asked ye
again, and Ken felt able to reassure him.

'I'm prepared to bet as much as sixpence that it will. An
takers?'

'Come on, Golly,' said Duffield. 'After all you've bee
saying, you must risk a bet.'

Golightly began to hedge, but a bet was finally arrangec
He staked one penny that they would not both reach th
top and keep out of the mist all day. Terms having bee
settled, Golightly set off at a cracking pace, whilst Ken wa
inclined to linger.

'Shall we take a look at the kennels of the Ullswate
hounds?' he asked. 'There's no violent hurry, you know.

Golightly pretended not to hear, plugging upwards in a
endeavour to disappear into the clouds so that he coul
claim his penny. The clouds, however, had a distinct tendenc
to lift, and more and more of the long slope of Birkhous
Moor, up which the path went, came into view.

'It isn't fair, we ought to have started earlier,' grumble
Golightly.

188

'We might have done if you hadn't played silly b's with your shoes,' said Ken.

'Please, sir, what's a silly b?' asked Anderson.

'Golightly was – when he lost his shoe,' countered Mike, and there the matter rested.

For the best part of an hour they toiled upwards, until they came to a wall. The path went through a gap in this wall, and Ken declared a halt. Golightly seemed upset, feeling that any delay was grossly unfair.

'Now look here, Golly, we don't want to muck around Striding Edge in the mist. We're having a rest here, and then going down to Red Tarn for our meal. We'll see what the weather's like then. You still win your wretched penny if we don't get to the top, you know.'

Golightly cheered up at this, but Stevenson's face fell a mile. It would be too hard to bear if they turned back now.

Red Tarn is in a kind of crater, nestling between Striding Edge and Swirral Edge. Its waters were unruffled by the wind which was blowing gustily around the party. All the boys, with one exception, were through the gap in the wall, gazing towards Striding Edge, which was still enshrouded in mist.

'That's odd,' said Ken, as he looked around, 'very odd indeed.'

'What is?' asked Ann.

'I smell smoke. Who's missing?'

'We're short of Macpherson.'

'So we are,' said Ken, still sniffing.

He crept cautiously back to the gap in the wall, putting his head quietly round the corner. There was Macpherson puffing away at a cigarette.

'Put that bonfire out, Macpherson,' he said, 'and give me the packet.'

'Yes, sir,' said a very crestfallen Macpherson.

'Do your parents allow you to smoke?'

'I don't think so, sir.'

'I don't think I do either. Really, you do look damned silly.'

Ken smoked himself, so he could hardly give a convincing lecture on the danger to health. It was a little pointless too to spin the old yarn that smoking stunted the growth or ruined the lungs. Macpherson already weighed well over ten stone, and he was supremely fit. The fifteen-hundred-foot slog up the path had been nothing to him, nor would the scramble to the top, either, with or without the aid of cigarettes.

'And Macpherson, don't smoke again this trip, or I really shall be cross.'

'No, sir.'

'Right.'

Ken and the erring Macpherson rejoined the main force and Ken set off for Red Tarn.

'*En avant, mes braves,*' he said. 'Lunch interval as soon as we get there.'

There was an undignified scramble, and the seven younger members of the expedition reached the luncheon place some time before the lunch itself.

12

An hour later, they had eaten their meal and scrambled round the tarn without anyone falling in, by which time it was obvious that the improvement in the weather was something more than a temporary lull. There were still ragged banners of mist, which made Striding Edge all the more exciting, and Golightly had a financial interest in getting in amongst them. He set off towards the heights with a grim determination, a quality needed as he was still enveloped in complete storm gear. All the others had abandoned theirs, so, before the start of the scramble Ken called upon him to divest himself of his cape and leggings. It was blowing quite hard on the ridge, and a cape could be dangerous.

'Remove them, Golly,' he called out. 'If you get caught in a gust of wind, you'll take off.'

'But, sir, it's the easiest way to carry it all.'

Ken had a quick look round, and saw that the other six were somewhat cluttered up with their impedimenta. It would be as well if they all had both hands free.

'OK,' he said, 'I'll take the lot in my rucksack. This isn't going to be dangerous, but you've got to take care.'

There was a pause whilst the gear was collected up and stowed. Ken asked Ann to lead and Mike to take up the rear, whilst he stationed himself in a strategic central position. They had barely reached the interesting part of the climb when Golightly began to experience trouble with his nether garments.

'I say, sir,' he said to Mike, 'my trousers seem to be falling, down.'

191

Mike stayed with him whilst he adjusted his clothing which naturally took up a certain amount of time. Being neither an elegant nor a swift mover, Golightly was unable to close the gap which had opened up, and he and Mike became detached from the main body. They had proceeded perhaps fifty yards along the ridge, when once again Golightly had to stop for repairs.

'What seems to be the trouble, my friend?' asked Mike

'It's this belt, sir.'

'Pity you aren't wearing braces.'

'I was yesterday, sir.'

'Well, you've chosen a poorish spot for experimenting with a belt.'

'Two buttons came off my trousers on High Street, sir so I had to try my belt.'

'If they come down again, you'll have to take them of altogether.'

After this dire threat, they proceeded towards a patch of mist.

'Just look at that, sir. If we can reach it, my penny's safe.

They did reach it, and became engulfed. This caused so much pleasure to Golightly that he failed to concentrate sufficiently on the upkeep of his trousers. They began to slide gracefully down his abdomen, having paused momentarily at its most protruding part. His shape was such that his hips were no earthly use as a stopper. At a particularly tricky portion of the ridge, Golightly lost all control of them and the offending garments sank to his ankles.

'Right, take them off,' said Mike.

'Oh no, sir,' said Golightly, outraged at the very thought of such an indignity.

'Oh yes, sir,' said Mike firmly, and Golightly stepped coyly out of them and handed them over.

The sight of his rotund figure appearing out of the mist in his underpants was greeted, with surprise and then a evity which Golightly himself considered to be misplaced. He snatched back his property, and reclothed himself with some haste. At the top of the path, near a monument to a climber whose whole person as well as his trousers had fallen down, the faulty belt was repaired with string, and Golightly claimed from Mike the penny which he had won.

'But I've not been in the mist yet,' said Ken.

True enough, no one but the rearguard had been affected, but eventually Ken paid up. From his enthusiasm, one would have thought that Golightly had gained one of the larger Premium Bond prizes. For Stevenson, it was a triumph too, and all the way down Swirral Edge, up to the top of Catstycam and down into Keppelcove, where tea was taken, he never stopped congratulating himself on his remarkable achievement. The boys played by the stream which runs through the broken dam. There wasn't very much water – but Anderson fell in.

The following day was a Friday, when the Wintergreen expedition left in peace the warden of Patterdale to inflict itself on an area further west. Three nights is considered quite long enough for any one Youth Hostel to put up with its guests, so a move was forced upon them. Leaving a no doubt jubilant Patterdale before ten o'clock, they had nowhere to rest their weary heads before the doors of Eskdale Hostel opened to receive them that evening. Although in those days it was not strictly according to the rules for the White Spider to be used at all, Ken had no hesitation in bending them to his advantage.

'If it's quite legal to take a bus or thumb a lift, I don't see why we shouldn't use our own transport,' he said. 'Anyway, by the end of the day we shall have covered a hell of a lot more of the fells on our flat feet than some members of some school parties do during their entire stay in the Lake District.'

In this, he was not far wrong, for they managed a very good ten miles before they sank onto the cushions of their faithful steed. According to Smythe's journal, which is quoted verbatim, the major summit of the day was Fairfield.

> Lefte hostel at nine-thirty. To tope of Fairfield (2863 feet). Went by Deepdale and Greenhow End. Weather lovely. Back to Patterdale by Cofa Pike, smashing scramble, and St Sunday Crag. Don't no who St Sunday was, nor did Kenny. Dinner at Deepdale Hause. Swapped corned dog for lemone curd sandwich.

They were back in Patterdale before four, and Ken showed a certain amount of impatience in getting all aboard.

'What's the hurry, sir?' asked Duffield. 'It can't be much more than twenty miles to Eskdale.'

'It isn't, but you just look at the map again.'

'Hmm, I see what you mean, sir,' said Duffield learnedly. 'Kirkstone Pass (one thousand four hundred and eighty nine feet) between us and Ambleside. That's quite a climb.'

'It is. Now go on, past Skelwith Bridge and onto the western half of the map.'

'I've got it, sir – Wrynose Pass (one thousand two hundred and eighty-one feet).'

'Yes, that's even worse, even if it's not so high.'

'Oh, and sir, there's Hardknott Pass too. One thousand two hundred and ninety-one feet.'

'Yes, you can't fail to notice that; it's the worst of the lot. You may all have to push me up that one.'

As a matter of fact, they didn't, but the White Spider had shown a certain amount of distress going up the Wrynose Pass, so Ken decanted the party at the foot of Hardknott and made them walk up after him.

'It'll wear the stiffness off,' he told Golightly, when that young gentleman expressed serious doubts about his ability to reach the top under his own steam.

'You'll never do it, sir,' said Macpherson despairingly.

'You've said that twice already.'

'I know, but look at those bends.'

'You watch us,' said Ken. 'We'll be tired of waiting for you.'

The White Spider took heart at shedding its load of a good half-ton of live weight. It juddered protestingly on the corners, but reached the top all right.

'I told you it would be all right,' said Ken with some pride, as Macpherson reached him. He was the first of the walkers, and well ahead of the field.

'It's a miracle, sir. What's the time?'

'About six, I should think. Why?'

'Will we be able to have a look at the camp?'

'Mediobogdum? I should think so; supper at Eskdale isn't until seven-thirty.'

On a moderately level spur of the mountain, perhaps halfway down the pass, are the ruins of a Roman fort. Its name, Mediobogdum, had already attracted the attention of the boys, and Golightly's translation – 'The fort in the middle of the bogs' – was considered the height of wit. The wretched Roman soldiers, particularly those who came from pleasant Mediterranean climes, probably saw little to laugh at when they were stationed there. Admiring the excellent view, whenever the weather permitted, must have palled after a time, and the only other entertainment offered them was an hour or two in the Roman baths, whose remains are still to be seen outside the very imposing walls of the encampment. Even the less historically minded of the boys were prepared to listen to Ken's ten-minute lecture before they wandered round on their own. After the examination, Duffield had a pertinent question to ask.

'What on earth did they use that gate for, sir?' he said, pointing across to the far side of the fort.

'For getting in and out of the fort, of course.'

This was considered a point against the expert, and Duffield was mocked.

'Very funny,' he continued, 'but it leads straight on to a very steep slope.'

'Handy for a rubbish tip,' said Mike.

'It seems a bit silly to me, sir.'

'But Roman forts always did have at least one gateway on each of their four sides. Even those on Hadrian's Wall did,' continued Ken.

'What's the reason, sir? One would have been quite enough here.'

'Bureaucracy, my dear Duffer. Some blinking civil servant in Rome drew up the plan for a fort, and that was that.'

'Nobody seemed to show much initiative, sir.'

'Maybe not, but it has its advantages, you know.'

'I suppose you mean that the Romans could just get to work on the fort without having to do much thinking.'

'Yes – and so can the archaeologists now. They've only to spot one corner of a fort, and they know where to dig for the rest of it – from the CO's residence to the troops' latrines.'

The inspection over, the interest of everyone switched to the hostel and supper. None of the staff had been there recently, and they were agreeably surprised to see one major change. They had expected oil lamps and candles, but electricity had now reached far enough up the valley to be of service to the hostellers.

'What a pity,' said Ann, 'I should like to have seen Golightly retiring upstairs to bed by candlelight.'

The boys themselves were disappointed. They could not quite visualise the difficulties of a dozen people undressing by the light of one candle, and it might perhaps have been of educational value if they could have been given the experience.

The stay at Eskdale was an unqualified success, though the Sunday excursion had to be modified on account of the weather. It was Wilkinson's opinion that this was because a visit to church had not been arranged, and that the Almighty had kept the clouds at a uniform nine hundred feet as a mark of His displeasure. Saturday, however, was glorious. The programme was a long trip up the dale, taking in the tops of Crinkle Crags and Bowfell. Both are mountains of great character, and from them the views across to the Scafell range are superb. The Crinkles must be the knobbliest collection of tops in the whole Lake District; Mr Wainwright lists five main summits, but Golightly had counted up to double figures long before the party had finished with them. From the top of Bowfell to the dining-room at Eskdale Hostel is a very long way, and it was supper time as the tailenders staggered up the drive.

That evening, in the bar of the Woolsack, Ken broached the subject of the excursion for the following day.

'I don't know what you think,' he said, 'but I'm all for having a crack at Scafell Pike tomorrow.'

'They've had a bit of a hammering today. Do you think they can take it?' asked Ann.

'When it comes to climbing the highest mountain in England, they'll take it all right.'

'But I thought we were doing Scafell Pike from the other side when we were staying in Keswick,' said Mike.

'That was the idea, I know, but we ought to make the best use of the weather. It may break by the time we get round to Keswick.'

'Right, I'm game,' said Mike, and Ann agreed.

'I think we might keep this under our hats,' went on

197

Ken. 'We don't want to disappoint young Stevenson. He
hasn't yet grasped that there's anything higher than Helvellyn
outside the Himalayas. When he does know, there'll be no
holding him until he's been to the top.'

It was just as well that they had decided on this action
for Sunday dawned windy and wet. The clouds were not
too low, but something less ambitious than Scafell Pike was
clearly indicated. Even the top of Harter Fell, at just over
two thousand feet, was covered in clouds.

'Let's go over into Wasdale over Burnmoor,' said Mike.

'By the old corpse road?'

'Ooh, sir, why is it a corpse road?' asked several voices
at once.

When they heard that anyone being inconsiderate enough
to die in Wasdale used to have to be carried over Burnmoor
for Christian burial, the boys decided unanimously that
nothing could give them greater pleasure than to go over
the route in the opposite direction. What is more, they
started up a doleful dirge as soon as they left the hostel
precincts, and kept it up intermittently until Wasdale was
in sight. Either the comfort which they gained from this
dreary pastime or else the inclement weather caused them
to move at some considerable speed, and they had reached
the shores of Wastwater at least half an hour before lunch
could decently be taken.

'If we stop now, Anderson's sure to fall in, and it will be
darned cold anyhow,' said Mike.

'What about taking the path by the lakeside?' asked Ann.
'We might find some shelter amongst the boulders where
it peters out.'

'I doubt it – but it's an idea anyway,' was Ken's verdict
and the party set out.

The truck at the foot of Wasdale Screes is, for all but a
fraction of its length, a perfectly normal lakeside path. With
the mountain rising abruptly above it, broken cliffs at the

op and acres and acres of scree below, it is an exciting walk, but over most of it an agile grandmother could be taken without adverse comment either from her or from anyone else. There is, however, one alarming quarter-mile section where the path just cannot cope with the terrain. The walker suddenly finds himself having to fight his way across a belt of huge jumbled boulders; it is a very formidable obstacle, for the path ceases to exist. Ann thought that possibly amongst the boulders a nook could be found, a shelter from what could justifiably be called the stormy blast. When they got there, it was patently obvious that no such nook existed, but a hurried lunch was eaten, and the journey continued before any of the party froze up. Their next port of call was a power station at the end of the lake where, by standing alongside some ventilators, it was possible to find comfort from the warm air which was being expelled. There, a council of war was held. It had by this time stopped raining, and there seemed to be no clouds covering the top of the Screes.

'Now what would you like to do, lads?' asked Ken. 'We've got to keep moving, or we'll freeze up. We can take in a couple of tops if we go up by the side of that ravine, or else walk back into Eskdale by a very pleasant path which keeps fairly low. We'll even split up into two parties if you like.'

'Let's go up, sir,' said Macpherson, squaring his broad shoulders.

'Let's stay down, sir,' said Golightly firmly.

After further discussion, a vote was taken, and only Golightly wished to avoid the steep and rugged pathway to the tops.

'Right you are, Golly,' said Ken. 'We'll put you on your way. Duffer will lend you his map, and you can't go wrong.'

'Wait a bit, sir,' said Duffield. 'You don't know Golly like me. I'll stay with him and look after him.'

199

SCOTT COOPER

'Good. I must say I'd prefer it that way myself.'

'We'll come and look for you, sir, if you get lost.'

'That's a relief, it restores my confidence.'

After detailed instructions, the 'B' party set out, no one expecting to see them again before they reached the hostel. The mountaineers eventually reached the top of the Screes and were suitably impressed by the views down to the lake. The clouds were just above their heads, and the wind whistled round them, but they were well protected. It took some time for them to walk along the top, and for Burnmoor to come in sight again, at which Wilkinson remarked that the corpse road would not be quite the same without Golightly's doleful voice to lead them.

'But we aren't going that way, we're going down Miterdale,' said Ken.

Miterdale is a valley which few can have explored unless, of course, they have studied Mr Wainwright's *Southern Fells*. It starts very close indeed to the desolate Burnmoor Tarn, but one would never suspect it existed if one did not know already. When the party descended into its secret recesses, they felt as if they had discovered an unknown hiding place. It was therefore both surprising and slightly annoying that they should find the hollow already occupied. Golightly and Duffield, looking very excited, were awaiting their descent, obviously with important news.

'Sir,' they announced together, 'you must come with us, we've found a train.'

'Good,' said Ken, 'lead us to it, and we'll return it to British Rail.'

'But it isn't theirs,' said Duffield. 'We must hurry, or we'll miss it.'

Eventually, it transpired that the 'B' party had indeed found a train. As they were hustling along their path, they had heard a whistle in the distance. On investigating Irton Road, they had unearthed one of the more important

200

stations of the Ravenglass and Eskdale Railway, and they had discovered from the timetable that a train would be stopping there at five o'clock on its way up to the terminus at Dalegarth. Now Dalegarth was no more than a long mile from the hostel, and Duffield decided that the Wintergreen Expedition must catch that train. Knowing that Ken was leading his lot down Miterdale, he and Golightly had charged up to meet them. So hot was their pace, and so accurate Duffield's map reading, that they reached the head of the dale some thirty seconds before the mountaineers.

'OK,' said Ken, after everything had been made clear, 'do you want a trip on the train?'

'Oh yes, sir,' came in chorus.

'Right, we should just about make it.'

Actually, they had no great difficulty in reaching the station in time. After a five-minute wait, distant puffing was heard, and soon an engine, the *River Irt* by name, came importantly round the bend. It was towing a collection of minute carriages, and it did not seem to realise that its funnel reached no higher than the driver's midriff, as he sat at the controls. It was supporting to great effect the majesty of steam, when a rival concern had cravenly gone over to stinking and characterless diesel.

'I'm paying extra and going first class,' said Duffield grandly. He stepped into the only coach with windows, whilst his companions clambered up into open carriages. The trip lasted a quarter of an hour at most, but Stevenson put the experience at least on a level with the ascent of Helvellyn.

On Monday, the move to the third and final hostel had to be made. As before, the White Spider was illicitly employed, but the party paused at Loweswater to climb Mellbreak, a mountain of no great height but with a soul as great as the

River Irt. They had a magnificent scramble up the northern end, walked along the top and descended by one of the steepest grass slopes in the area. Golightly it was who discovered that his cape could be used as a kind of toboggan; Anderson it was who left his toboggan far astern, removing in the process both the entire seat of his trousers and a largish area of skin from his bottom. At Low Ling Crag, Ken said that anyone who wanted a bathe could have one. He did not expect anyone to take up the offer, but Smythe and Wilkinson cast off their clothes madly, plunged into the iciness of Crummock Water and shot out almost as quickly as they had dived in. As Ann said afterwards, they were hardly in long enough to pollute the Whitehaven water supply.

From Loweswater, the White Spider went to Buttermere, and then valiantly over Newlands Hause and down the valley to the fleshpots of Keswick. Soon the expedition was walking along the wooden platform above the river, the only method of reaching the haven where they would be – the Fitzpark Hostel.

'Not spud bashing again, I hope,' said Mike, as they waited whilst Ken signed them in.

All the time that they had been at Eskdale, the duty of the Wintergreen contingent had been the peeling of potatoes for the evening meal. After a short period of initial chaos, a system had been evolved whereby the boys did some preliminary excavations on the virgin spuds. They then dropped what they considered to be their masterpieces into a fresh bucket, generally from a great height, and the adults took over. In theory, the staff had simply to remove minor blemishes, but the efforts of the boys were not always a wild success. Wilkinson, being artistic, was apt to use the potatoes as material for sculpture, and Anderson secretly carved 'A's on his to see whether he could identify his own handiwork at table. At the end of the proceedings, the party was forced to mop up both the floor, if the duty was done indoors, and themselves anyway. It was exhausting work, and the fact that the warden praised then for their tireless devotion to duty and for the excellence of the finished article was small consolation for the hard labour and the major discomfort involved.

Previously, at Patterdale, their work had not been as laborious for the staff, but it was far less to the taste of the boys. There, washing-up was their daily portion, and, in comparing the two, they quickly appreciated that a dropped potato cost nothing, whilst a dropped cup did. Poor Golightly lost the best part of a day's pocket money before he was transferred by common consent to the sweeping out of the dormitory. There, he managed to surround himself with a dense cloud of dust, but the room was even more sordid after he had finished his administrations than before he had started them. Mike found it necessary to clean up after him, and he maintained that it was very much harder to make an engineering job after Golightly's efforts than if that maid of all work had been sent out with his brush for a short walk.

But spud peeling at Keswick was a gentleman's pursuit, for a machine performed the dirty work and all that the human element was called upon to do was to eye the otherwise finished article, washing-up, too, was a simple job, no fewer than twenty bodies sharing the work. There were, however, larger parties of bigger pupils, and the Wintergreeners were given a variety of lesser chores. They were submerged, if boys of the calibre of Golightly and Anderson ever can be submerged, by two large mixed groups, one cockney and the other Lancastrian in origin. Of these, one was tough in the extreme, but the other appeared to have done nothing but loaf in the streets of Keswick and Ambleside. Ann slept in the same room as a mistress from this party, and was amazed by her attitude. It seemed that she had signed on for the trip simply so that she could add Youth Hostelry with her charges as a further qualification should she seek employment elsewhere. Fortunately, ladies of her kind and parties like her party are rare.

The weather, having started to pick up on Monday, now decided that it was time to stage a positively idyllic period. The sun shone in a cloudless sky, there was a nice little breeze to freshen up foot travellers and the mountains looked their very best.

'We'll do Scafell Pike today,' announced Ken after breakfast, and the White Spider was soon on the way up Borrowdale to Seathwaite.

It was one of those expeditions which go well from the start. At Stockley Bridge, which marks the real beginning of the climb, they all paused for elevenses, and then the assault began. Climbing by Grains Gill and Ruddy Beck, two names to gladden the heart of any Lake District lover, even Golightly seemed to be going like a bomb.

'Please, sir,' he said on hearing the name of the latter stream, 'why's it a ruddy beck?'

'Because it's ruddy steep,' answered Smythe, who had chosen a poor route and was somewhat puffed.

'Not quite,' said Ken. 'You'll see why when we get a bit higher. The soil at the top is red – like blood.'

The boys hurried upwards with some enthusiasm.

'Please, sir,' asked Stevenson, after they had admired the most satisfactorily red stains, and a huge chunk of mountain obscured the view ahead, 'is that Scafell Pike?'

'No,' answered Mike, 'it's Great End.'

'Yes, it is, sir, but what's it called?'

'It's called Great End, Stevenson. That's its name.'

'Funny name for a mountain.'

'Well, can you think of a better one?' asked Ken. 'It is a great end, isn't it? We've a long way to go before we even see the top of Scafell Pike.'

Instead of groans, which would have been the normal reaction, the party just set its teeth and increased the pace. It was not really so very long afterwards before the top did come in sight, although it was still a longish way off. There were jumbled boulders reminiscent of the path by Wastwater, and a couple of dips before the final scramble to the top, but they got there without incident.

'My feet are the highest in England,' said Anderson, doing a handstand, at which he was most proficient, on the summit cairn.

'What, sir,' said Duffield to Ken, 'is your usual procedure when you reach the top of a mountain?'

'Why, if I've forgotten to bring a flag, I kiss the nearest pretty girl,' answered Ken, suiting the action to the words and taking Ann in his arms.

The boys were highly delighted, but for some reason Mike was not all that enthusiastic. It gave him considerable food for thought, in fact, and his mind was not entirely on the job in hand as they set out for Mickledore and the neighbouring summit of Scafell.

Scafell Pike and Scafell are two separate mountains not more than three-quarters of a mile apart as the crow flies, but between them is a great gulf fixed. At Mickledore, the lowest part of the ridge connecting the two, three possible routes can be taken. To the right, involving a further dip before an eight hundred-foot climb to the top of Scafell, lies Lord's Rake; to the left, an even greater loss of height leads to a less well-known path by Foxes Tarn. Both these are scrambles that anyone can manage without too much fear of vertigo and sudden death, but straight ahead lies Broad Stand. This, the great Mr Wainwright states, is not for walkers – and he is perfectly right. The actual barrier, however, a barrier which has defeated so many in its time, is one short pitch of a few feet. With the aid of one competent climber and another agile assistant, Ken had no hesitation in choosing this route. He shepherded his charges onto a ledge, and passed them into the waiting hands of Mike and Ann to everyone's entire satisfaction. His was by no means the first prep school party which had been helped up Broad Stand in this way.

Before they reached the top of Scafell, Mike braced himself for a repetition of the scene which had shaken him on the Pike. Fortunately, Ann kept well clear of Ken, and anyway he showed no signs of wishing to repeat the performance. They stayed on the top for a good ten minutes, for the view was superb and the weather warm enough for them to admire it without any discomfort. Then Ken reminded them that they had still six long mountain miles to go.

'Do we sweat up Scafell Pike again, sir?' asked Golightly.

'No, it's a different route all the way, and there's not so very much more climbing.'

'That's fine, sir, I'm about jiggered,' said Golightly with obvious relief.

'Nonsense, you can't feel tired once we've started – it's the finest walk in England,' said Ken.

Golightly was more than a little sceptical, but he enjoyed the switchback descent of Lord's Rake. However, the scree down to the climbers' traverse below the Pulpit Rock taxed his capabilities to the utmost, and the effort required to hoist himself to the top of Lingmell Col seemed enormous to him. After that, it was easier going, even his tired legs deciding to function without too much agony. The Corridor Route to Styhead was sheer delight, whilst the scramble down the path at Taylor Gill Force was a better way of losing height than most.

Mike could never really remember at what point he finally decided that he must propose to Ann, but it was somewhere on the Corridor Route. His first opportunity did not occur until nearly the end of the descent by Taylor Gill Force. He took it. There was a wall, which the rest of the party crossed, leaving Ann and Mike on the further side. By the time that Anderson had re-climbed this obstruction in order to seek cover for a very necessary purpose, it was obvious that Mike had both popped the question and had it satisfactorily answered. With no embarrassment whatever, they all told each other what they were going to do and, when Anderson was able to rejoin the main body, he it was who announced the engagement.

'I say,' he shouted, 'sir's going to marry Miss Pinkerton.'

'Which sir?' asked Golightly, looking puzzled. Mr Padgett's activities on the mountain top could well be a prelude to matrimony, and yet here was Mr Thornton looking thoroughly soppy and holding Miss Pinkerton's hand. All very confusing for a chap who openly admitted that he had rather more stomach than brain, but his doubts were cleared up by Ken.

'Not me, surely,' he said, with a look of horror on his face. He had every intention of remaining a bachelor for some considerable time to come.

'Certainly not,' said the hand-holders in unison.

The rest of the holiday had, for Mike and Ann anyway, a certain dreamlike quality. It was Duffield who insisted that an engagement ring must be bought the very next day.

'Now, sir,' he said firmly even before they had returned to base at Seathwaite, 'what about an engagement ring?'

'Well, I don't know...' started Mike.

'You've got to give her one; it's obligatory.'

'I am aware of the procedure, Duffield.'

Duffield pulled him aside, and with the greatest tact asked him about his financial situation. He felt that it was tantamount to living in sin if no ring could be shown to Matron at the end of the trip. So great were his powers of persuasion that he forced Mike into agreement.

'No ring, no engineering job, you think?' asked Mike at last.

'Definitely, sir.'

'OK, do you think that two pounds eleven and six will do?' he asked, after making a rapid mental calculation.

'Is that all you've got, sir? What about the Post Office Savings Bank?'

'My book's at home.'

'That seems rather imprudent, sir, if I may say so. You should always carry it with you. Never mind, I'll negotiate a loan.'

That evening, he collected up twenty-three shillings from the boys and two promises of a fiver each when the post office opened from Ken and Ann. What sort of a yarn he spun to the last-named is a closely guarded secret, but it was not until Mike was slipping a ring, neat but not gaudy, on her finger that she realised that she was paying for well over a third of it herself.

Business having been transacted, the party had an hour on the lake. The boatman insisted, and quite rightly, that there should be an adult in each boat, but he made the mistake of putting Macpherson into the adult category so that the party could be spread out into four boats. With Duffield and Golightly as crew, he proceeded in voluptuous curves, followed by ever-diminishing circles. At the end of the hour, his boat was towed back ignominiously by Ken, or it would still, at this very moment, constitute a slow-moving danger to navigation.

The sun continued to shine, and a leisurely ascent of Skiddaw filled in the remainder of the day. Golightly and the White Spider attained about nine hundred and fifty feet, at which point the former lay comfortably down in the latter, to dream peacefully about food, and other pleasant things. Smythe and Wilkinson were overcome by exhaustion halfway up Jenkin Hill, and strolled down after an hour or two to interrupt Golightly's snores. Anderson and Duffield stopped at the two thousand foot mark, and were picked up later on the return journey whilst earnestly attempting to teach an elderly and rather bored sheep to beg for some milk chocolate. Ann and Mike turned aside at Little Man, whose secluded summit was rather more to their taste, so three only of the party were left to carry the Wintergreen colours to the top of Skiddaw. Of these, Macpherson and Ken were hardly tired, and Stevenson had little difficulty in making it when he realised that this was the last of the three-thousand-footers in the Lake District. He had done the lot, and was inordinately pleased with himself.

And so to the day of departure. Any ordinary people would have driven straight back home after such an exhausting week, but Blencathra rose temptingly on the left, and it was a nice clear day. They climbed it, and Golightly managed Sharp Edge, a rival to the more famous Striding Edge, without losing his trousers. It then seemed a pity to drive back straight to school, and they remembered that Matron had instructed them to make a pilgrimage to the churchyard at Caldbeck. In order not to incur her displeasure, they turned aside off the main Penrith road. A beautiful bunch of daffodils, obviously collected illicitly by Golightly, was placed reverently at the foot of John Peel's grave, and Ken hustled them away without enquiring too closely into the origin of this touching floral tribute.

At ten o'clock that night, a tired and dishevelled carload of mountaineers arrived at the school. Matron was there to welcome them. She congratulated Ann and Mike, but told them they were far too young to get spliced. They could only agree with her, and say that their engagement would be a long one. Having scrubbed the boys with ardour, Matron then tucked them up smartly in bed. Needless to say, she made an engineering job of it.

209